London

$9\frac{1}{4}$

findin

$9\frac{1}{4}$

THE BIG BOOK
OF ANIMAL STORIES

THE BIG BOOK OF ANIMAL STORIES

COMPILED AND EDITED BY
MARGARET GREEN

PICTURES BY
JANUSZ GRABIANSKI

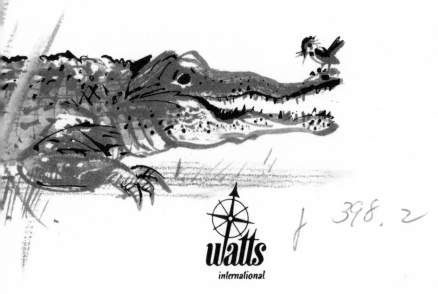

f 398. 2

watts
international

FRANKLIN WATTS · INC.
575 LEXINGTON AVENUE · NEW YORK CITY

First American publication, 1961, by Franklin Watts, Inc.

First published in Great Britain in 1961 by Dobson Books Ltd.,
80 Kensington Church Street, London W 8

Illustrations: © 1961 by Carl Ueberreuter Druck und Verlag (M. Salzer),
Vienna, Austria

Printed by Carl Ueberreuter Druck und Verlag (M. Salzer), Vienna, Austria

FOURTH PRINTING

ACKNOWLEDGMENTS

The editor and the publisher have made every effort to trace the ownership of all material contained herein. It is their belief that the necessary permissions from publishers, authors, and authorized agents have been obtained in all cases. In the event of any question arising as to the use of any material, the editor and publisher, while expressing regret for any error unconsciously made, will be pleased to make the necessary correction in future editions of this book. Thanks are due the following authors, publishers, publications, and agents for permission to use the material indicated.

Farrar, Straus and Cudahy, Inc., for "The Lost Leg," from *The Adventure of Maya the Bee,* by Waldemar Bonsels, copyright 1951, by Waldemar Bonsels.

Doubleday and Company, Inc., for "The Elephant's Child," from *Just So Stories,* by Rudyard Kipling. Reprinted by permission of Doubleday and Company, Inc., A. P. Watt and Son, the Macmillan Company of Canada, and Mrs. George Bambridge; for "The Wonderful Adventures of Nils," from *The Wonderful Adventures of Nils* by Selma Lagerlöf. © Copyright 1907 by Doubleday and Company, Inc. Reprinted by permission.

Franklin Watts, Inc., for "Not Quite Martin," from *This Boy Cody,* by Leon Wilson. © Copyright 1950 by Leon Wilson.

The American Folklore Society, Inc., for "Tar Baby," contributed by Miss Dora Lee Newman to *Marion County in the Making* (privately printed), 1918, and reprinted in *The Journal of American Folklore,* Vol. 47, 1934.

Flensted, Odense, for "The Ugly Duckling," from *Hans Christian Andersen, Fairy Tales,* translated by R. P. Keigwin, copyright 1950, bei Flensted.

Franklin Watts, Inc., for "Clever Brother Hare," from *Fairy Tales From Many Lands,* copyright 1956, by Franklin Watts, Inc., for "Little Half-Chick," from *The First Book of Fairy Tales,* retold by Elizabeth Abell, copyright 1958, by Franklin Watts, Inc.

Oxford University Press, England, for "A Bridegroom for Miss Mouse," from *Burmese Folk Tales,* by Maung Htin Aung, copyright 1948, by Oxford University Press.

U. S. 1538592

CONTENTS

ABOUT THESE STORIES:

THIS is a book about animals who think and talk and behave like people. The tradition is an old one; as old, in fact, as the serpent who talked with Eve. And unless we manage, in this age of the machine, to divorce ourselves completely from the world of wonder, animals will probably go right on thinking and talking and behaving in ways they were never meant to.

Some of the oldest talking animal stories are myths in which men once tried to explain their own beginnings in terms of the animals who were on earth before them. Such a tale is the Miwok Indian story of the coyote who created man.

Many students of folklore believe that the talking-animal stories were originally meant for grownups. Surely the myths were, and also many of those stories that point a moral or satirize human mannerisms, such as the fables of Aesop, or the Burmese folk tale, "A Bridegroom for Miss Mouse." That these stories are enjoyed chiefly by children today in no way detracts from their charm and wisdom.

The origins of most of the old talking-animal stories are lost, and so it is interesting to see the same stories appearing in different parts of the world. The details of these stories may differ, but the plots and meanings remain the same.

It is also interesting to see how closely the animals, for all their human actions, resemble their living counterparts. The fox (or his cousin, the jackal) is weak, and must rely on his wits to win. The lion is king of the beasts. The dog is the friend of man, while the cat walks alone in his mystery and intelligence. Nowhere, even in realistic fiction, is the cat better portrayed than in that wonderful and strangely mysterious old tale called "King O' the Cats," where Master Tom confounds his human protectors by making a human pronouncement before taking off on his great adventure.

If there are less solemn things to say about animal stories written primarily to amuse little children, we must at least admit that they are true to the nature of childhood. It is quite natural for animals to talk to us when we are young, and quite natural for us to understand them. Children know instinctively that animals are people in disguise, to be protected and indulged as later the grown-up child will protect and indulge small beings of his own kind.

This collection pretends to be no more than a sampling of the thousands of stories about animals who behave like human beings. Some, like the story of the three little pigs and the wolf, will be familiar to most people. Many readers will also recognize the story of the ugly duckling, presented here in a new and faithful translation by R. P. Keigwin. Other stories may be less familiar, and one, the story of the crab and the crane, has not, to the knowledge of this editor, been set down in English before. It was told to the writer by a homesick boy from Egypt, working behind an American soda fountain.

Margaret Green

THE THREE LITTLE PIGS

This is a just-for-fun folk tale that has delighted generations of children. It is English.

ONCE upon a time there were three little pigs whose mother was so poor she did not have enough to feed them. So one day she sent them out into the world to seek their fortunes.

The first little pig met a man with a bundle of straw and said to him, "Please give me that straw so that I can build myself a house."

The man gave him the straw, and the little pig built a house with it.

The little pig was very happy in his new house until a wolf came along and knocked at the door and said, "Little pig! Little pig! Let me in!"

The little pig answered, "No, no, by the hair of my chinny chin chin."

"Then I'll huff and I'll puff and I'll blow your house in," said the wolf. And he huffed and he puffed and he blew the house in. The little pig ran away as fast as he could so that the wolf would not eat him up.

The second little pig met a man with a load of wood

and said to him, "Please give me that wood so that I can build myself a house."

The man gave him the wood, and the little pig was just building a house with it when along came the first little pig who had just run away from the wolf. Together they built a house of wood, but no sooner had they finished it than the wolf came again. He knocked at the door and said, "Little pigs, little pigs, let me come in!"

The second little pig answered, "No, no, no, by the hair of my chinny chin chin."

"Then I'll huff and I'll puff and I'll blow your house in," said the wolf.

And he huffed and he puffed, and he puffed and he huffed, and he blew the house in. The two little pigs ran away as fast as they could.

The third little pig met a man with a load of bricks

and said to him, "Please give me those bricks so that I can build myself a house."

The man gave him the bricks, and the little pig was just building a house with them when along came the first little pig with the second little pig. They had just run away from the wolf. All three little pigs began to build as fast as they could, but no sooner had they finished the house than the wolf arrived outside. He knocked at the door and said, "Little pigs, little pigs, let me come in!"

The third little pig answered, "No, no, by the hair of my chinny chin chin."

"Then I'll huff and I'll puff and I'll blow your house in," said the wolf.

And he huffed and he puffed, and he puffed and he huffed, but he could not blow the house in. The three little pigs rejoiced and thought they were quite safe now.

But the wolf was really angry because he could not blow the house in, and he was also very hungry. He simply must catch those three little pigs! He thought a long time, then climbed up to the roof of the house and tried to get down the chimney. Luckily for the three little pigs, he slipped and fell right into a pot of boiling water that was hanging over the fire.

When the three little pigs saw what had happened, they quickly put the cover on the pot, boiled the wolf up, and ate him for supper and then they lived happily in their little brick house ever after.

A MAD TEA-PARTY

by LEWIS CARROLL

If you enjoy this story, you will probably want to read the rest of Alice in Wonderland, *a book about a little girl who fell down a rabbit hole into a queer, topsy-turvy land.*

THERE was a table set out under a tree in front of the house, and the March Hare and the Hatter were having tea at it: a Dormouse was sitting between them, fast asleep, and the other two were using it as a cushion, resting their elbows on it, and talking over its head.

"Very uncomfortable for the Dormouse," thought Alice; "only as it's asleep, I suppose it doesn't mind."

The table was a large one, but the three were all crowded together at one corner of it. "No room! No room!" they cried out when they saw Alice coming.

"There's *plenty* of room!" said Alice indignantly, and she sat down in a large arm-chair at one end of the table.

"Have some wine," the March Hare said in an encouraging tone.

Alice looked all round the table, but there was nothing on it but tea. "I don't see any wine," she remarked.

"There isn't any," said the March Hare.

"Then it wasn't very civil of you to offer it," said Alice angrily.

"It wasn't very civil of you to sit down without being invited," said the March Hare.

"I didn't know it was *your* table," said Alice: "it's laid for a great many more than three."

"Your hair wants cutting," said the Hatter. He had been looking at Alice for some time with great curiosity, and this was his first speech.

"You should learn not to make personal remarks," Alice said with some severity: "it's very rude."

The Hatter opened his eyes very wide on hearing this; but all he said was, "Why is a raven like a writing-desk?"

"Come, we shall have some fun now!" thought Alice.

15

"I'm glad they've begun asking riddles—I believe I can guess that," she added aloud.

"Do you mean that you think you can find out the answer to it?" said the March Hare.

"Exactly so," said Alice.

"Then you should say what you mean," the March Hare went on.

"I do," Alice hastily replied; "at least—at least I mean what I say—that's the same thing, you know."

"Not the same thing a bit!" said the Hatter. "Why, you might just as well say that 'I see what I eat' is the same thing as 'I eat what I see'!"

"You might just as well say," added the March Hare, "that 'I like what I get' is the same thing as 'I get what I like'!"

"You might just as well say," added the Dormouse, which seemed to be talking in its sleep, "that 'I breathe when I sleep' is the same thing as 'I sleep when I breathe'!"

"It *is* the same thing with you," said the Hatter, and here the conversation dropped, and the party sat silent for a minute, while Alice thought over all she could remember about ravens and writing-desks, which wasn't much.

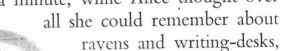

The Hatter was the first to break the silence. "What day of the month is it?" he said, turning to Alice: he had taken his watch out of his pocket, and was looking at it uneasily, shaking it every now and then, and holding it to his ear.

Alice considered a little, and then said, "The fourth."

"Two days wrong!" sighed the Hatter. "I told you butter wouldn't suit the works!" he added, looking angrily at the March Hare.

"It was the *best* butter," the March Hare meekly replied.

"Yes, but some crumbs must have got in as well," the Hatter grumbled: "you shouldn't have put it in with the bread-knife."

The March Hare took the watch and looked at it gloomily: then he dipped it into his cup of tea, and looked at it again: but he could think of nothing better to say than his first remark, "It was the *best* butter, you know."

Alice had been looking over his shoulder with some curiosity. "What a funny watch!" she remarked. "It tells the day of the month, and doesn't tell what o'clock it is!"

"Why should it?" muttered the Hatter. "Does *your* watch tell you what year it is?"

"Of course not," Alice replied very readily: "but that's because it stays the same year for such a long time together."

"Which is just the case with *mine*," said the Hatter.

Alice felt dreadfully puzzled. The Hatter's remark

17

seemed to her to have no sort of meaning in it, and yet it was certainly English. "I don't quite understand you," she said, as politely as she could.

"The Dormouse is asleep again," said the Hatter, and he poured a little hot tea upon its nose.

The Dormouse shook its head impatiently, and said, without opening its eyes, "Of course, of course; just what I was going to remark myself."

"Have you guessed the riddle yet?" the Hatter said, turning to Alice again.

"No, I give it up," Alice replied. "What's the answer?"

"I haven't the slightest idea," said the Hatter.

"Nor I," said the March Hare.

Alice sighed wearily. "I think you might do something better with the time," she said, "than wasting it in asking riddles that have no answers."

"If you knew Time as well as I do," said the Hatter, "you wouldn't talk about wasting *it*. It's *him*."

"I don't know what you mean," said Alice.

"Of course you don't!" the Hatter said, tossing his head contemptuously. "I dare say you never even spoke to Time!"

"Perhaps not," Alice cautiously replied; "but I know I have to beat time when I learn music."

"Ah! That accounts for it," said the Hatter. "He won't stand beating. Now, if you only kept on good terms with him, he'd do almost anything you liked with the clock. For instance, suppose it were nine o'clock in the morning, just time to begin lessons: you'd only have to whisper a hint to Time, and round goes the clock in a twinkling! Half-past one, time for dinner!"

("I only wish it was," the March Hare said to itself in a whisper.)

"That would be grand, certainly," said Alice thoughtfully; "but then—I shouldn't be hungry for it, you know."

"Not at first, perhaps," said the Hatter: "but you could keep it to half-past one as long as you liked."

"Is that the way *you* manage?" Alice asked.

The Hatter shook his head mournfully. "Not I!" he replied. "We quarreled last March—just before *he* went mad, you know—" (pointing with his teaspoon at the March Hare) "—it was at the great concert given by the

19

Queen of Hearts, and I had to sing

'Twinkle, twinkle, little bat!
How I wonder what you're at!'

You know the song, perhaps?"

"I've heard something like it," said Alice.

"It goes on, you know," the Hatter continued, "in this way:—

'Up above the world you fly,
Like a tea-tray in the sky.
Twinkle, twinkle—'"

Here the Dormouse shook itself, and began singing in its sleep *"Twinkle, twinkle, twinkle, twinkle—"* and went on so long that they had to pinch it to make it stop.

"Well, I'd hardly finished the first verse," said the Hatter, "when the Queen bawled out, 'He's murdering the time! Off with his head!'"

"How dreadfully savage!" exclaimed Alice.

"And ever since that," the Hatter went on in a mournful tone, "he won't do a thing I ask! It's always six o'clock now."

A bright idea came into Alice's head. "Is that the reason so many tea-things are put out here?" she asked.

"Yes, that's it," said the Hatter with a sigh: "it's always tea-time, and we've no time to wash the things between whiles."

"Then you keep moving round, I suppose?" said Alice.

"Exactly so," said the Hatter: "as the things get used up."

"But when you come to the beginning again?" Alice ventured to ask.

"Suppose we change the subject," the March Hare interrupted, yawning. "I'm getting tired of this. I vote the young lady tells us a story."

"I'm afraid I don't know one," said Alice, rather alarmed at the proposal.

"Then the Dormouse shall!" they both cried. "Wake up, Dormouse!" And they pinched it on both sides at once.

The Dormouse slowly opened its eyes. "I wasn't

asleep," it said in a hoarse, feeble voice, "I heard every word you fellows were saying."

"Tell us a story!" said the March Hare.

"Yes, please do!" pleaded Alice.

"And be quick about it," added the Hatter, "or you'll be asleep again before it's done."

"Once upon a time there were three little sisters," the Dormouse began in a great hurry; "and their names were Elsie, Lacie, and Tillie; and they lived at the bottom of a well—"

"What did they live on?" said Alice, who always took a great interest in questions of eating and drinking.

"They lived on treacle," said the Dormouse, after thinking a minute or two.

"They couldn't have done that, you know," Alice gently remarked: "they'd have been ill."

"So they were," said the Dormouse; "*very* ill."

Alice tried a little to fancy to herself what such an extraordinary way of living would be like, but it puzzled her too much: so she went on: "But why did they live at the bottom of a well?"

"Take some more tea," the March Hare said to Alice, very earnestly.

"I've had nothing yet," Alice replied in an offended tone: "so I can't take more."

"You mean you can't take *less*," said the Hatter: "it's very easy to take *more* than nothing."

"Nobody asked *your* opinion," said Alice.

"Who's making personal remarks now?" the Hatter asked triumphantly.

Alice did not quite know what to say to this: so she helped herself to some tea and bread-and-butter, and then turned to the Dormouse, and repeated her question. "Why did they live at the bottom of a well?"

The Dormouse again took a minute or two to think about it, and then said "It was a treacle well."

"There's no such thing!" Alice was beginning very angrily, but the Hatter and the March Hare went "Sh! Sh!" and the Dormouse sulkily remarked "If you can't be civil, you'd better finish the story for yourself."

"No, please go on!" Alice said very humbly. "I won't interrupt you again. I dare say there may be *one*."

"One, indeed!" said the Dormouse indignantly. However, he consented to go on. "And so these three little sisters—they were learning to draw, you know—"

"What did they draw?" said Alice, quite forgetting her promise.

"Treacle," said the Dormouse, without considering at all, this time.

"I want a clean cup," interrupted the Hatter: "let's all move one place on."

He moved on as he spoke, and the Dormouse followed him: the March Hare moved into the Dormouse's place, and Alice rather unwillingly took the place of the March Hare. The Hatter was the only one who got any advantage from the change; and Alice was a good deal worse off than before, as the March Hare had just upset the milk-jug into his plate.

Alice did not wish to offend the Dormouse again, so she began very cautiously: "But I don't understand. Where did they draw the treacle from?"

"You can draw water out of a water-well," said the Hatter; "so I should think you could draw treacle out of a treacle-well—eh, stupid?"

"But they were *in* the well," Alice said to the Dormouse, not choosing to notice this last remark.

"Of course they were," said the Dormouse:—"well in."

This answer so confused poor Alice, that she let the Dormouse go on and on without interrupting it.

"They were learning to draw," the Dormouse went

on, yawning and rubbing its eyes, for it was getting very sleepy; "and they drew all manner of things — everything that begins with an M—"

"Why with an M?" said Alice.

"Why not?" said the March Hare.

Alice was silent.

The Dormouse had closed its eyes by this time, and was going off into a doze; but, on being pinched by the Hatter, it woke up again with a little shriek, and went on: "—that begins with an M, such as mouse-traps, and the moon, and memory, and muchness—you know you say things are 'much of a muchness'—did you ever see such a thing as a drawing of a muchness!"

"Really, now you ask me," said Alice, very much confused, "I don't think—"

"Then you shouldn't talk," said the Hatter.

This piece of rudeness was more than Alice could bear:
she got up in great disgust, and walked off: the Dormouse
fell asleep instantly, and neither of the others took the
least notice of her going, though she looked back once
or twice, half hoping that they would call after her:
the last time she saw them, they were trying to put the
Dormouse into the teapot.

"At any rate I'll never go *there* again!" said Alice, as
she picked her way through the wood. "It's the stupidest
tea-party I ever was at in all my life!"

THE FOX AND THE GEESE
by JAKOB AND WILHELM GRIMM

Jakob and Wilhelm Grimm were two learned men of Germany who loved the old myths and folk tales so dearly that they put many of them into books for children to enjoy.

THE fox once came to a meadow in which there was a flock of fine fat geese. He smiled at them and said, "I came in the nick of time. You are sitting together quite beautifully, so that I can eat you up one after the other."

27

The geese cackled with terror, sprang up, and began to plead for their lives. But the fox would listen to nothing and said, "There is no mercy to be had! You must die!"

At last one of the geese got up the courage to say, "If we poor geese are to be eaten up by you, please let us make one more prayer so that we shall not die without having our sins forgiven. Then we shall all sit down in a row so that you can pick yourself the fattest first."

"Well," said the fox, "that seems like a reasonable request. Pray away. I shall not eat you until you are finished."

Then the first goose began a good long prayer, forever saying, "Ga! Ga!" And since she would not stop, the second did not wait her turn but joined her own, "Ga! Ga!" to the first. The third and fourth joined her, and soon they were all cackling together.

When the geese have finished praying, we shall go on with the story, but at this moment they are still praying without stopping!

THE LOST LEG

by WALDEMAR BONSELS

*Maya was a young bee who left the hive to see the world. On
her travels she met most of the creatures of the fields and woods.
Among them was Fridolin, a bark beetle, who introduced her
to a strange, long-legged animal who talked like a professor.*

"SEE who's coming," Fridolin cried, "coming up the
tree! Here's the fellow for you, I tell you, he's a—but
you'll see."

Maya followed the direction of his gaze and saw a
remarkable animal slowly climbing up the trunk. She
wouldn't have believed such a creature was possible if
she had not seen it with her own eyes.

"Hadn't we better hide?" she asked, alarm getting the better of astonishment.

"Absurd," replied the barkbeetle. "Just sit still and be polite to the gentleman. He is very learned, really, very scholarly, and what is more, he is kind and modest and rather funny. See what he's doing now!"

"Probably thinking," observed Maya, who couldn't get over her astonishment.

"He's struggling against the wind," said Fridolin, and laughed. "I hope he doesn't tangle his legs."

"Are those long threads really his legs?" asked Maya. "I've never seen the like."

Meanwhile the newcomer had drawn near, and Maya got a better view of him. He looked as though he were swinging in the air, his round little body hung so high on his monstrously long legs which groped for a footing on all sides like a movable scaffolding of threads. He stepped along cautiously, feeling his way. The little brown sphere of his body rose and sank, rose and sank. His legs were so very long and thin that one alone could certainly not have supported his body. He needed all his legs at once. As they were jointed in the middle, they rose high in the air above him.

Maya clapped her hands together.

"Well!" she cried. "Did you ever? Would you have dreamed that such delicate legs, legs as fine as a hair, could be so nimble and useful—that one could really use them—and they'd know what to do? Fridolin, I think it's wonderful, simply wonderful."

"Ah, bah," said the barkbeetle. "Don't take things so seriously. Just laugh when you see something funny; that's all."

By this time the stranger had joined them and was looking down at Maya from the height of his pointed triangles of legs.

"Good morning," he said, "a real wind storm—a pretty strong breeze, don't you think, or—no? You are of a different opinion?" He clung to the tree as hard as he could.

Fridolin turned to hide his laughter, but little Maya replied politely that she quite agreed with him and that was why she had not gone out flying. Then she introduced herself. The stranger squinted down at her through his legs.

"Maya, of the nation of bees," he repeated. "Delighted, really. I have heard a good deal about bees. I myself belong to the general family of spiders, Daddy-long-legs, first name Hannibal."

The word spider has an evil sound in the ears of all smaller insects, and Maya could not quite conceal her fright. Hannibal seemed to take no notice, so Maya decided, "Well, if need be, I'll fly away, and he can whistle for me. He has no wings, and his web is some-where else."

"I am thinking," said Hannibal, "thinking very hard. If you will permit me, I will come a little closer. That big branch there makes a good shield against the wind."

"Why, certainly," said Maya, making room for him.

Fridolin said good-by and left. Maya stayed because she was eager to understand Hannibal's personality.

"The many, many different kinds of animals there are in the world," she thought. "Every day a fresh discovery."

The wind had lessened somewhat, and the sun shone through the branches. From below rose the song of a robin redbreast, filling the woods with joy. Maya could see the bird perched on a branch, could see its throat swell and pulse with the song as it held its little head raised up to the light.

"If only I could sing like that robin redbreast," she said, "I'd perch on a flower and keep it up the livelong day."

"You'd produce something lovely, you would, with your humming and buzzing," said Daddy-long-legs.

"The bird looks so happy."

"You have great imagination," said Daddy-long-legs. "Supposing every animal were to wish he could do something that nature had not fitted him to do, the

world would be all topsy-turvy. Supposing a robin redbreast thought he had to have a sting—a sting above everything else—or a goat wanted to fly about gathering honey. Supposing a frog were to come along and wish for my kind of legs."

Maya laughed.

"That isn't just what I mean. I mean, it seems lovely to be able to make all beings as happy as the bird does with his song. But goodness gracious!" she exclaimed suddenly. "Mr. Hannibal, you have one leg too many."

Hannibal frowned and looked into space, annoyed.

"Well, you've noticed it," he said glumly. "But as a matter of fact—one leg too few, not too many."

"Why? Do you usually have eight legs?"

"Permit me to explain. We spiders have eight legs. We need them all. Besides, eight is a more aristocratic number. One of my legs got lost. Too bad about it. However you manage, you make the best of it."

"It must be dreadfully disagreeable to lose a leg," Maya sympathized.

Hannibal propped his chin on his hand and arranged his legs to keep them from being easily counted.

"I'll tell you how it happened. Of course, as usual when there's mischief, a human being is mixed up in it. We spiders are careful and look what, we're doing, but human beings are careless. They grab you sometimes as though you were a piece of wood. Shall I tell you?"

"Oh, do please," said Maya, settling herself comfortably. "It would be awfully interesting. You must certainly have gone through a good deal."

"I should say so," said Hannibal. "Now listen. We Daddy-long-legs, you know, hunt by night. I was then living in a green garden-house. It was overgrown with ivy, and there were a number of broken window panes, which made it very convenient for me to crawl in and out. The man came at dark. In one hand he carried his artificial sun, which he calls a lamp, in the other hand a small bottle, and under his arm some paper. He put everything down on the table and began to think, because he wanted to write his thoughts on the paper. You must certainly have come across paper in the woods or in the garden. The black on the paper is what man has excogitated—that means to think, you know."

"Wonderful!" cried Maya, all aglow that she was learning so much.

"For this purpose," Hannibal continued, "man needs a bottle. He inserts a stick into the bottle and makes

marks on the paper with the stick. Of course it is about us insects that he writes, everything he knows about us, and he writes very hard, but the result is not much to boast of, because up to now man has found out very little about insects. He knows nothing about our hearts, and hasn't the least consideration for our feelings. You'll see."

"Don't you like human beings?" asked Maya.

"Oh, yes, yes. But the loss of a leg"—Daddy-long-legs looked down slantwise—"is apt to embitter one, rather."

"I see," said Maya.

"One evening I was sitting on a window frame as usual, prepared for the chase, and the man was sitting at the table, his bottle before him, trying to produce something. It annoyed me dreadfully that a whole swarm of little flies and gnats, upon which I depend for my food, had settled upon the artificial sun and were staring into it in that stupid, uneducated way of theirs."

"Well," said Maya, "I think I'd look at a thing like that myself."

"Look, for all I care. But to look and to stare like an idiot are two entirely different things. Just watch once and see the silly jig they dance around a lamp. It's nothing for them to butt their heads about twenty times. Some of them keep it up until they burn their wings. And all the time they stare and stare at the light."

"Poor things! Evidently they lose their wits."

"Then they had better stay outside on the window frame or under the eaves. They're safe from the lamp

there, and that's where I can catch them. Well, on that
fateful night I saw from my position on the window
frame that some gnats were lying scattered on the table
beside the lamp, drawing their last breath. The man
did not seem to notice or care about them, so I decided
to go and take them myself. That's perfectly natural,
isn't it?"

"Perfectly."

"And yet, it was my undoing. I crept up the leg
of the table, very softly, on my guard, until I could
peep over the edge. The man seemed dreadfully big.
I watched him working. Then, slowly, very slowly,
carefully lifting one leg at a time, I crossed over to the
lamp. As long as I was hidden by the bottle, all went
well, but I had scarcely turned the corner when the
man looked up and grabbed me. He lifted me by one

of my legs, dangled me in front of his huge eyes, and said: 'See what's here, just see what's here.' And he grinned—the brute! He grinned with his whole face, as though it were a laughing matter."

Hannibal sighed, and little Maya kept quite still. Her head was in a whirl.

"Have human beings such immense eyes?" she asked at last.

"Please think of me in the position I was in," cried Hannibal, vexed. "Try to imagine how I felt. Who'd like to be hanging by the leg in front of eyes twenty times as big as his own body and a mouth full of gleaming teeth, each fully twice as big as himself? Well, what do you think?"

"Awful! Perfectly awful!"

"Thank goodness, my leg broke off. There's no telling what might have happened if my leg had not broken off. I fell to the table, and then I ran, I ran as fast as my remaining legs would take me, and hid behind the bottle. There I stood and hurled threats of violence at the man. They saved me, my threats did, the man was afraid to run after me. I saw him lay my leg on the white paper, and I watched how it wanted to escape— which it can't do without me."

"Was it still moving?" asked Maya, prickling at the thought.

"Yes. Our legs always do move when they're pulled out. My leg ran, but I not being there, it didn't know where to run to, so it merely flopped about aimlessly on the same spot, and the man watched it, clutching at his nose and smiling—smiling, the heartless wretch!— at my leg's sense of duty."

"Impossible," said the little bee, quite scared, "an offen leg can't crawl."

"An offen leg? What is an offen leg?"

"A leg that has come off," explained Maya, staring at him.

"You should drop your baby slang when you're out in the world and in the presence of educated people," said Hannibal severely. "But it is true that our legs totter long after they have been torn from our bodies."

"I can't believe it without proof."

"Do you think I'll tear one of my legs off to satisfy you?" Hannibal's tone was ugly. "I see you're not a fit person to associate with. Nobody, I'd like you to know, nobody has ever doubted my word before."

Maya was terribly put out. She couldn't understand

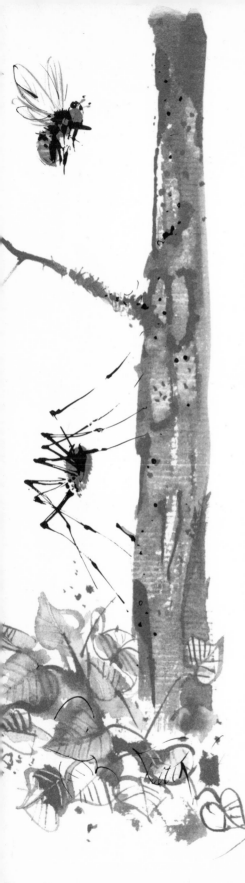

what had upset Daddy-long-legs so, or what dreadful thing she had done.

"It isn't altogether easy to get along with strangers," she thought. "They don't think the way we do and don't see that we mean no harm." She was depressed and cast a troubled look at Daddy-long-legs with his long legs and sour expression.

"Really, someone ought to come and eat you up," said Daddy-long-legs.

Hannibal had evidently mistaken Maya's good nature for weakness. For now something unusual happened to the little bee. Suddenly she was not afraid. She straightened up, lifted her lovely, transparent wings, uttered her high, clear buzz, and said with a gleam in her. eyes, "I am a bee, Mr. Hannibal."

"I beg your pardon!" said he, and without saying good-by, turned and ran down the tree trunk as fast as a person can run who has seven legs.

42

THE ELEPHANT'S CHILD
by RUDYARD KIPLING

*Did you ever wonder why the elephant has a long trunk? If you
read this story, you will learn the reason.*

IN the High and Far-Off Times the Elephant, O Best
Beloved, had no trunk. He had only a blackish, bulgy
nose, as big as a boot, that he could wriggle about
from side to side; but he couldn't pick up things with
it. But there was one Elephant—a new Elephant—an
Elephant's Child—who was full of 'satiable curtiosity,
and that means he asked ever so many questions. *And*
he lived in Africa, and he filled all Africa with his 'satiable

curtiosities. He asked his tall aunt, the Ostrich, why her tail-feathers grew just so, and his tall aunt, the Ostrich, spanked him with her hard, hard claw. He asked his tall uncle, the Giraffe, what made his skin spotty, and his tall uncle, the Giraffe, spanked him with his hard, hard hoof. And still he was full of 'satiable curtiosity! He asked his broad aunt, the Hippopotamus, why her eyes were red, and his broad aunt, the Hippopotamus, spanked him with her broad, broad hoof; and he asked his hairy uncle, the Baboon, why melons tasted just so,

and his hairy uncle, the Baboon, spanked him with his hairy, hairy paw. And *still* he was full of 'satiable curtiosity. He asked questions about everything that he saw, or heard, or felt, or smelt, or touched, and

all his uncles and his aunts spanked him. And still he was full of 'satiable curtiosity!

One fine morning in the middle of the Precession of the Equinoxes this 'satiable Elephant's Child asked a new fine question that he had never asked before. He asked, "What does the Crocodile have for dinner?" Then everybody said, "Hush!" in a loud and dretful tone, and they spanked him immediately and directly, without stopping, for a long time.

By and by, when that was finished, he came upon Kolokolo Bird sitting in the middle of a wait-a-bit thorn-bush, and he said, "My father has spanked me, and my mother has spanked me: all my aunts and uncles have spanked me for my 'satiable curtiosity; and *still* I want to know what the Crocodile has for dinner!"

The Kolokolo Bird said, with a mournful cry, "Go to the banks of the great gray-green, greasy Limpopo River, all set about with fever trees, and find out."

That very next morning, when there was nothing left of the Equinoxes, because the Precession had preceded according to precedent, this 'satiable Elephant's Child took a hundred pounds of bananas (the little, short, red kind), and a hundred pounds of sugar-cane (the long purple kind), and seventeen melons (the greeny-crackly kind), and said to all his dear families, "Good-bye. I am going to the great gray-green, greasy Limpopo River, all set about with fever trees, to find out what the Crocodile has for dinner." And they all spanked him once more for luck, though he asked them most politely to stop.

Then he went away, a little warm, but not at all astonished, eating melons, and throwing the rind about, because he could not pick it up.

He went from Graham's Town to Kimberley, and from Kimberley to Khama's Country, and from Khama's Country he went east by north, eating melons all the time, till at last he came to the banks of the great gray-green, greasy Limpopo River, all set about with fever trees, precisely as Kolokolo Bird had said.

Now you must know and understand, O Best Beloved, that till that very week, and day, and hour, and minute, this 'satiable Elephant's Child had never seen a Crocodile,

and did not know what one was like. It was all his 'satiable curtiosity.

The first thing that he found was a Bi-Coloured-Python-Rock-Snake curled round a rock.

"'Scuse me," said the Elephant's Child most politely, "but have you seen such a thing as a Crocodile in these promiscuous parts?"

"*Have* I seen a Crocodile?" said the Bi-Coloured-Python-Rock-Snake, in a voice of dretful scorn. "What will you ask me next?"

"'Scuse me," said the Elephant's Child, "but could you kindly tell me what he has for dinner?"

Then the Bi-Coloured-Python-Rock-Snake uncoiled himself very quickly from the rock, and spanked the

Elephant's Child with his scalesome, flailsome tail.

"That is odd," said the Elephant's Child, "because my father and my mother, and my uncle and my aunt, not to mention my other aunt, the Hippopotamus, and my other uncle, the Baboon, have all spanked me for my 'satiable curtiosity—and I suppose this is the same thing."

So he said good-bye very politely to the Bi-Coloured-Python-Rock-Snake, and helped to coil him up on the rock again, and went on, a little warm, but not at all astonished, eating melons, and throwing the rind about, because he could not pick it up, till he trod on what he thought was a log of wood at the very edge of the great gray-green, greasy Limpopo River, all set about with fever trees.

But it was really the Crocodile, O Best Beloved, and the Crocodile winked one eye—like this!

"'Scuse me," said the Elephant's Child most politely, "but do you happen to have seen a Crocodile in these promiscuous parts?"

Then the Crocodile winked the other eye, and lifted half his tail out of the mud; and the Elephant's Child stepped back most politely, because he did not wish to be spanked again.

"Come hither, Little One," said the Crocodile. "Why do you ask such things?"

"'Scuse me," said the Elephant's Child most politely, "but my father has spanked me, my mother has spanked me, not to mention my tall aunt, the Ostrich, and my tall uncle, the Giraffe, who can kick ever so hard, as

well as my broad aunt, the Hippopotamus, and my hairy uncle, the Baboon, *and* including the Bi-Coloured-Python-Rock-Snake, with the scalesome, flailsome tail, just up the bank, who spanks harder than any of them; and *so*, if it's quite all the same to you, I don't want to be spanked any more."

"Come hither, Little One," said the Crocodile, "for I am the Crocodile," and he wept crocodile-tears to show it was quite true.

Then the Elephant's Child grew all breathless, and panted, and kneeled down on the bank and said, "You are the very person I have been looking for all these long days. Will you please tell me what you have for dinner?"

"Come hither, Little One," said the Crocodile, "and I'll whisper."

Then the Elephant's Child put his head down close to the Crocodile's musky, tusky mouth, and the Crocodile caught him by his little nose, which up to that very week, day, hour, and minute, had been no bigger than a boot, though much more useful.

"I think," said the Crocodile—and he said it between

his teeth, like this—"I think to-day I will begin with Elephant's Child!"

At this, O Best Beloved, the Elephant's Child was much annoyed, and he said, speaking through his nose, like this, "Led go! You are hurtig be!"

Then the Bi-Coloured-Python-Rock-Snake scuffled down from the bank and said, "My young friend, if you do not now, immediately and instantly, pull as hard as ever you can, it is my opinion that your acquaintance in the large-pattern leather ulster" (and by this he meant the Crocodile) "will jerk you into yonder limpid stream before you can say Jack Robinson."

This is the way Bi-Coloured-Python-Rock-Snakes always talk.

Then the Elephant's Child sat back on his little haunches, and pulled, and pulled, and pulled, and his nose began to stretch. And the Crocodile floundered into the water, making it all creamy with great sweeps of his tail, and *he* pulled, and pulled, and pulled.

And the Elephant's Child's nose kept on stretching;
and the Elephant's Child spread all his little four legs
and pulled, and pulled, and pulled, and his nose kept on
stretching; and the Crocodile threshed his tail like an
oar, and *he* pulled, and pulled, and pulled, and at each
pull the Elephant's Child's nose grew longer and longer—
and it hurt him hijjus!

Then the Elephant's Child felt his legs slipping, and he said through his nose, which was now nearly five feet long, "This is too butch for be!"

Then the Bi-Coloured-Python-Rock-Snake came down from the bank, and knotted himself in a double-clove-hitch round the Elephant's Child's hind-legs, and said, "Rash and inexperienced traveller, we will now seriously devote ourselves to a little high tension, because if we do not, it is my impression that yonder self-propelling man-of-war with the armour-plated upper deck" (and by this, O Best Beloved, he meant the Crocodile) "will permanently vitiate your future career."

That is the way all Bi-Coloured-Python-Rock-Snakes always talk.

So he pulled, and the Elephant's Child pulled, and the Crocodile pulled; but the Elephant's Child and the

Bi-Coloured-Python-Rock-Snake pulled hardest; and at last the Crocodile let go of the Elephant's Child's nose with a plop that you could hear all up and down the Limpopo.

Then the Elephant's Child sat down most hard and sudden; but first he was careful to say "Thank you" to the Bi-Coloured-Python-Rock-Snake; and next he was kind to his poor pulled nose, and wrapped it all up in cool banana leaves, and hung it in the great gray-green, greasy Limpopo to cool.

"What are you doing that for?" said the Bi-Coloured-Python-Rock-Snake.

"'Scuse me," said the Elephant's Child, "but my nose is badly out of shape, and I am waïting for it to shrink."

"Then you will have to wait a long time," said the Bi-Coloured-Python-Rock-Snake. "Some people do not know what is good for them."

The Elephant's Child sat there for three days waiting for his nose to shrink. But it never grew any shorter, and, besides, it made him squint. For, O Best Beloved, you will see and understand that the Crocodile had pulled it out into a really truly trunk same as all Elephants have to-day.

At the end of the third day a fly came and stung him on the shoulder, and before he knew what he was doing he lifted up his trunk and hit that fly dead with the end of it.

"'Vantage number one!" said the Bi-Coloured-Python-Rock-Snake. "You couldn't have done that with a mere-smear nose. Try and eat a little now."

Before he thought what he was doing the Elephant's Child put out his trunk and plucked a large bundle of grass, dusted it clean against his fore-legs, and stuffed it into his own mouth.

"'Vantage number two!" said the Bi-Coloured-Python-Rock-Snake. "You couldn't have done that with a mere-smear nose. Don't you think the sun is very hot here?"

61

"It is," said the Elephant's Child, and before he thought what he was doing he schlooped up a schloop of mud from the banks of the great gray-green, greasy Limpopo, and slapped it on his head, where it made a cool schloopy-sloshy mud-cap all trickly behind his ears.

"'Vantage number three!" said the Bi-Coloured-Python-Rock-Snake. "You couldn't have done that with a mere-smear nose. Now how do you feel about being spanked again?"

"'Scuse me," said the Elephant's Child, "but I should not like it at all."

"How would you like to spank somebody?" said the Bi-Coloured-Python-Rock-Snake.

"I should like it very much indeed," said the Elephant's Child.

"Well," said the Bi-Coloured-Python-Rock-Snake, "you will find that new nose of yours very useful to spank people with."

"Thank you," said the Elephant's Child, "I'll remember that; and now I think I'll go home to all my dear families and try."

So the Elephant's Child went home across Africa, frisking and whisking his trunk. When he wanted fruit to eat he pulled fruit down from a tree, instead of waiting for it to fall as he used to do. When he wanted grass he plucked grass up from the ground, instead of going on his knees as he used to do. When the flies bit him he broke off the branch of a tree and used it as a fly-whisk; and he made himself a new, cool, slushy-squashy mud-cap whenever the sun was hot. When he felt lonely walking through Africa he sang to himself down his trunk, and the noise was louder than several brass bands. He went specially out of his way to find a broad Hippopotamus (she was no relation of his), and he spanked her very hard, to make sure that the Bi-Coloured-Python-Rock-Snake had spoken the truth about his new trunk. The rest of the time he picked up the melon rinds

64

that he had dropped on his way to the Limpopo—for he was a Tidy Pachyderm.

One dark evening he came back to all his dear families, and he coiled up his trunk and said, "How do you do?" They were very glad to see him, and immediately said, "Come here and be spanked for your 'satiable curtiosity."

"Pooh!" said the Elephant's Child. "I don't think you peoples know anything about spanking; but *I* do, and I'll show you."

Then he uncurled his trunk and knocked two of his dear brothers head over heels.

"O Bananas!" said they, "where did you learn that trick, and what have you done to your nose?"

"I got a new one from the Crocodile on the banks of the great gray-green, greasy Limpopo River," said the Elephant's Child. "I asked him what he had for dinner, and he gave me this to keep."

"It looks very ugly," said his hairy uncle, the Baboon.

"It does," said the Elephant's Child. "But it's very useful," and he picked up his hairy uncle, the Baboon, by one hairy leg, and hove him into a hornet's nest.

Then that bad Elephant's Child spanked all his dear families for a long time, till they were very warm and greatly astonished. He pulled out his tall Ostrich aunt's tail-feathers; and he caught his tall uncle, the Giraffe, by the hind-leg, and dragged him through a thorn-bush; and he shouted at his broad aunt, the Hippopo-tamus, and blew bubbles into her ear when she was sleeping in the water after meals; but he never let any-one touch Kolokolo Bird.

At last things grew so exciting that his dear families went off one by one in a hurry to the banks of the great gray-green, greasy Limpopo River, all set about with fever trees, to borrow new noses from the Croco-dile. When they came back nobody spanked anybody any more; and ever since that day, O Best Beloved, all the Elephants you will ever see, besides all those that you won't, have trunks precisely like the trunk of the 'satiable Elephant's Child.

THE WONDERFUL
ADVENTURES OF NILS
by SELMA LAGERLÖF

*This exciting story about young Nils' long, cold night spent up
in a birch-tree, outwitting clever Smirre Fox, has been popular
in Sweden for many years.*

AS the white goosey-gander sized up the wild geese, he
felt ill at ease. He had expected that they would be more
like tame geese, and that he would feel a closer kinship
with them. They were much smaller than he, and none of
them was white. All were gray with a sprinkling of brown.
He was almost afraid of their eyes, which were yellow
and shone as if a fire had been kindled behind them.
The goosey-gander had always been taught that it was
most fitting to move slowly and with a rolling mo-

tion, but these creatures did not walk — they almost ran. He grew most alarmed, however, when he looked at their feet. They were large, with torn and ragged-looking soles. It was apparent that the wild geese never questioned what they tramped upon. They took no by-paths. They were very neat and well cared for in other respects, but one could tell by their feet that they were poor wilderness-folk.

The goosey-gander only had time to whisper to the boy: "Speak up quickly for yourself, but don't tell them who you are!" — before the geese were upon them.

When the wild geese had stopped in front of them, they curtseyed with their necks many times, and the goosey-gander did likewise many more times. As soon as

the ceremonies were over, the leader-goose said: "Now I presume we shall hear what kind of creatures you are."

"There isn't much to tell about me," said the goosey-gander. "I was born in Skanör last spring. In the fall I was sold to Holger Nilsson of West Vemmenhög, and there I have lived ever since." "You don't seem to have any pedigree to boast of," said the leader-goose. "What is it, then, that makes you so high-minded that you wish to associate with wild geese?" "It may be because I want to show you wild geese that we tame ones may also be good for something," said the goosey-gander. "Yes, it would be well if you could show us that," challenged the leader-goose. "We have already observed how much you know about flying; but you are more skilled, perhaps, at other sports. Possibly you are strong in a swimming match?"

"No, I can't boast that I am," said the goosey-gander. It seemed to him as if the leader-goose had already made up her mind to send him home, so he didn't much care how he answered. "I never swam any farther than across a marl ditch," he retorted. "Then I presume you're a crack sprinter," said the goose. "I have never seen a tame goose run, nor have I ever done so myself," said the goosey-gander; and he made things appear much worse than they really were.

The big white one was sure now that the leader-goose would say that under no circumstances could they take him along. He was very much astonished when she said:

"You answer questions courageously; and he who has courage can become a good traveling companion, even if he is ignorant in the beginning. What do you say to stopping with us a couple of days, until we can see what you are good for?" "That suits me!" said the goosey-gander — and he was thoroughly happy.

Thereupon the leader-goose pointed with her bill and said: "But whom have you there? I've never seen any one like him before." "That's my comrade," said the goosey-gander. "He's been a goose-tender all his life. He'll be useful, all right, to take with us on the trip." "Yes, he may be all right for a tame goose," retorted the wild one. "What do you call him?" "He has several names," said the goosey-gander hesitatingly, not knowing what he should hit upon in a hurry, for he didn't want to reveal the fact that the boy had a human name. "Oh! his name is Thumbietot," he said at last. "Does he belong to the elf family?" asked the leader-goose. "At what hour do you wild geese usually retire?" said the goosey-gander quickly — trying to evade that last question. "My eyes close of their own accord about this time."

One could easily see that the goose who talked with the

gander was very old. Her entire feather outfit was ice-gray with no dark streaks. The head was larger than that of the others; the legs were coarser, and the feet were more worn. The feathers were stiff; the shoulders knotty; the neck thin. All this was due to age. It was only upon the eyes that time had had no effect. They shone brighter — as if they were younger than those of the others.

She turned very haughtily toward the goosey-gander. "Understand, Mr. Tame-goose, that I am Akka from Kebnekaise! And that the goose who flies nearest me — to the right — is Iksi from Vassijaure, and the one to the left is Kaksi from Nuolja! Understand, also, that the second right-hand goose is Kolmi from Sarjektjakko, and the second, left, is Neljä from Svappavaara; and behind them fly Viisi from Oviksfjällen and Kuusi from Sjangeli! And know that these, as well as the six goslings, who fly last — three to the right, and three to the left — are all high mountain geese of the finest breed! You must not take us for land-lubbers who strike up a chance acquaintance with any and every one! And you must not think that we permit anyone to share our quarters that will not tell us who his ancestors were."

While Akka, the leader-goose, was talking in this strain, the boy stepped briskly forward. It distressed him that the

goosey-gander, who had spoken up so glibly for himself, should give such evasive answers when it concerned him.

"I don't care to make a secret of who I am," said he. "My name is Nils Holgersson. I'm a farmer's son, and, until today, I was a human being; but this morning —" He got no further. As soon as he said that he was human the leader-goose staggered three steps backward, and the rest of them even farther back. All craned their necks and hissed angrily at him.

"I have suspected this ever since I first saw you here on these shores," said Akka: "and now you can clear out of here at once. We tolerate no human beings among us."

"It isn't possible," said the goosey-gander meditatively, "that you wild geese can be afraid of anyone who is so tiny! By tomorrow, of course, he'll turn back home. You can surely let him stay with us overnight. None of us can afford to let such a poor little creature wander off by himself in the night — among weasels and foxes!"

The wild goose came nearer. But one could see that it was hard for her to master her fear. "I have been taught to fear everything in human shape — be it big or little," said she. "But if you will answer for this one, and swear that he will not harm us, he may stay with us tonight. But I don't believe our night quarters are suitable for either him or you, for we intend to roost on the broken ice out here."

She thought, of course, that the goosey-gander would be doubtful when he heard this, but he never let on. "She is pretty wise who knows how to choose such a safe bed," said he.

"You will be answerable for his return to his own to-morrow."

"Then I, too, will have to leave you," said the goosey-gander. "I have sworn that I would not forsake him."

"You are free to fly whither you will," said the leader-goose.

With this, she raised her wings and flew out over the ice, and, one after another, the wild geese followed her.

The boy was very sad to think that his trip to Lapland would not come off, and, into the bargain, he was afraid of the chilly night quarter. "It will be worse and worse," said he. "In the first place, we'll freeze to death on the ice."

But the gander was in good humour. "There's no danger," he said. "Only make haste, I beg of you, and gather up as much grass and litter as you can well carry."

When the boy had an armful of dried grass, the goosey-gander grabbed him by the shirtband, lifted him, and flew out upon the ice, where the wild geese were already fast asleep with their bills tucked under their wings.

"Now spread out the grass on the ice so there will be something to stand on, to keep me from freezing fast. You help me and I'll help you," said the goosey-gander.

· This the boy did. And when he had finished, the goosey-gander again picked him up by the shirtband, and tucked him under his wing. "I think you'll lie snug and warm there," said the goosey-gander as he covered him with his wing.

The boy was so embedded in down that he couldn't answer; and he was nice and comfy. Oh, but he was tired! And in less than two winks he was fast asleep.

It is a fact that ice is always treacherous and not to be trusted. In the middle of the night the loosened icecake on Vomb Lake moved about, till one corner of it touched the shore. Now it happened that Mr. Smirre Fox, who lived at this time in Övid Cloister-Park — on the east side of the lake — caught a glimpse of that one corner while out on his night chase. Smirre had seen the wild geese early in the evening, and hadn't even dared to hope that he might get at one of them: but now he walked straight out on the ice.

When Smirre was very near to the geese, his claws scraped the ice, and the geese awoke, flapped their wings, and prepared for flight. But Smirre was too quick for them. He darted forward as though he'd been shot, grabbed a goose by the wing and ran toward land again.

But this night the wild geese were not alone on the ice, for they had a human being among them — little as he was. The boy had awakened when the goosey-gander spread his wings. He had tumbled down on the ice and was sitting there, dazed. He hadn't grasped the whys and wherefores of all this confusion until he had caught sight of a little long-legged dog who ran over the ice with a goose in his mouth.

In a second the boy was after that dog, to take the goose away from him. He must have heard the goosey-gander call to him: "Have a care, Thumbietot! Have a care!" But the boy thought that such a little runt of a dog was nothing to be afraid of, so he rushed ahead.

The wild goose that Smirre Fox was tugging along heard the clatter as the boy's wooden shoes beat against the ice, and she could hardly believe her ears. "Does that infant think he can take me away from the fox?" she wondered. And in spite of her misery, she began to cackle right merrily, deep down in her windpipe. It was almost as if she had laughed.

"The first thing he knows, he'll fall through a crack in the ice," thought she.

But dark as the night was, the boy saw distinctly all the cracks and holes there were, and took daring leaps over them. This was because he had the elf's good eyesight now, and could see in the dark. He saw both lake and shore just as clearly as if it had been daylight.

Smirre Fox left the ice where it touched the shore. And just as he was working his way up to the land-edge, the boy shouted to him: "Drop that goose, you sneak!" Smirre didn't know who was calling to him, and wasted no time in looking around, but increased his pace.

The fox made straight for the forest and the boy followed him, with never a thought of the risk he was running. On the contrary, he was thinking all the while about the contemptuous way in which he had been received by the wild geese that evening; and he made up his mind to let them see that a human being was something higher than all else created.

He shouted, again and again to that dog, to make him drop his game. "What kind of a dog are you, who can steal

a whole goose and not feel ashamed of yourself? Drop her at once! or you'll see what a beating you'll get. Drop her, I say, or I'll tell your master how you behave!"

When Smirre Fox saw that he had been mistaken for a fierce dog, he was so amused that he came near dropping the goose. Smirre was a great plunderer who wasn't satisfied with hunting only rats and pigeons in the fields, but he also ventured into the farmyards to steal chickens and geese. He knew that he was feared throughout the district; and anything so idiotic as this he had not heard since he was a baby.

The boy ran so fast that the thick beech trees appeared to be running past him — backward, and he gained on Smirre. Finally, he was so close to him that he got a hold on his tail. "Now I'll take the goose from you anyway," cried he, holding on as tight as ever he could, but he hadn't strength enough to stop Smirre. The fox dragged him along until the dry foliage whirled around him.

But now it began to dawn on Smirre how harmless was the creature that pursued him. He stopped short, put the goose on the ground, and held her down with his forepaws, so she couldn't fly away. He was just about to bite

off her neck — but he couldn't resist the desire to tease the boy a little. "Hurry off and complain to the master, for now I'm going to bite the goose to death!" said he.

Certainly the one who was surprised when he saw what a pointed nose, and heard what a hoarse and angry voice that dog that he was pursuing had, was — the boy! But now he was so provoked because the fox had made fun of him that he never thought of being frightened. He took a firmer hold on the tail, braced himself against a beech trunk; and just as the fox opened his jaws over the goose's throat, he pulled as hard as he could. Smirre was so astonished that he let himself be pulled backward a couple of steps — and the wild goose got away. She fluttered upward, feebly and heavily. One wing was so badly wounded that she could barely use it. Besides, she could not see in the night darkness of the forest, but was as helpless as the blind. Therefore she could in no way help the boy. She groped her way through the branches and flew down to the lake again.

Then Smirre made a dash for the boy. "If I don't get the one, I shall certainly have the other," said he; and you could tell by his voice how mad he was. "Oh, don't you believe it!" said the boy, who was in the best of spirits because he had saved the goose. He held himself fast by the foxtail, and swung with it to one side when the fox tried to catch him.

There was such a dance in that forest that the dry beech leaves fairly flew! Smirre swung round and round, but the tail swung too; while the boy kept a tight grip on it, so the fox couldn't grab him.

The boy was so gay after his success that, in the beginning, he only laughed and made fun of the fox. But Smirre
was persevering— as old hunters generally are — and the
boy began to fear that he would be captured in the
end.

Then he caught sight of a little, young beech tree that
had shot up as slender as a rod, that it might soon reach the
free air above the canopy of branches that the old beeches
spread over it.

Quick as a flash, he let go of the foxtail and climbed the beech tree. Smirre Fox was so excited that he continued to dance around after his tail a long time.

"Don't bother with the dance any longer!" said the boy.

But Smirre couldn't endure the humiliation of his failure to get the better of such a little tot, so he lay down under the tree, that he might keep a close watch on him.

The boy didn't have any too good a time of it where he sat, astride a frail branch. The young beech did not, as yet,

reach the high branch canopy, so the boy couldn't get over to another tree, and he didn't dare come down. He was so cold and numb that he almost lost his hold around the branch; and he was dreadfully sleepy; but he didn't dare fall asleep for fear of tumbling down.

My! but it was dismal to sit that way the whole night through, out in the forest! He had never before understood the real meaning of "night." It was just as if the whole world had become petrified, and never could come to life again.

Then it commenced to dawn. The boy was glad that everything began to look like itself once more; although the chill was even sharper than it had been during the night.

When the sun finally came up, it wasn't yellow but red. The boy thought it looked as if it was angry and he wondered what it was angry about. Perhaps it was because the night had made it so cold and gloomy on earth while the sun was away.

The sunbeams came down in great clusters, to see what the night had been up to. It could be seen how all things blushed — as if they all had guilty consciences. The clouds in the skies; the satiny beech limbs; the little intertwined branches of the forest canopy; the hoarfrost that covered the brushwood — everything grew flushed and red. More and more sunbeams came bursting through space, and soon the night's terrors were driven away, and such a marvelous lot of living things came forward. The black woodpecker, with the red neck, began to hammer with its bill on the branch. The squirrel glided from his nest with a nut, sat down on a branch and began to shell it. The starling came flying with a worm, and the bullfinch sang in the treetop.

Then the boy understood that the sun had said to all these tiny creatures: "Wake up now, and come out of your nests! I'm here! Now you needn't be afraid of anything."

The wild goose call was heard from the lake, as the geese were preparing for flight; and soon all the fourteen geese came flying through the forest. The boy tried to call to them, but they flew so high that his voice couldn't reach them. They probably believed the fox had eaten him up; and they didn't trouble themselves to look for him.

The boy came near crying with chagrin; but the sun stood up there — orange-faced and happy — and put courage into the whole world. "It isn't worth while, Nils Holgersson, for you to be troubled about anything, so long as I'm here," said the sun.

THE GOOSE CHASE

Everything remained unchanged in the forest about as long as it takes a goose to eat her breakfast. But just as the morning was verging on forenoon, a goose came flying, all by herself, under the thick tree canopy. She groped her way hesitatingly between stems and branches, and flew very slowly. As soon as Smirre Fox saw her, he left his place under the beech tree, and sneaked toward her. The wild goose didn't avoid the fox, but flew quite close to

him. Smirre made a high jump for her but missed her; and the goose went on her way, down to the lake.

It was not long until another goose came flying. She took the same route as the first one, and flew still lower and slower. She, too, flew close to Smirre Fox, and he made such a high spring for her that his ears brushed her feet. But she, too, got away from him unhurt, and went her way toward the lake, silent as a shadow.

A little while passed, and then along came another wild goose. She flew still slower and lower; and it seemed even more difficult for her to find her way between the beech branches. Smirre made a powerful spring! He was within a hair's breadth of catching her; but that goose also managed to save herself.

Just after she had disappeared, there came a fourth. She flew so slowly and so badly, that Smirre Fox thought he could catch her without much effort, but now he was afraid of failure and decided to let her fly past, unmolested. She took the same direction the others had taken; and just as she was right above Smirre, she sank down so

far that he was tempted to jump for her. He jumped so high that he touched her with his tail. But she flung herself quickly to one side, and saved her life.

Before Smirre had ceased panting, three more geese came flying in a row. They flew just like the rest, and Smirre made high springs for all three, but he did not succeed in catching one of them.

After that came five more geese; but these flew better than the others. And although it appeared as if they wanted to coax Smirre to jump, he withstood the temptation. After quite a long time came one lone goose. It was the thirteenth. This one was so old that she was gray all over, without a dark speck anywhere on her body. Apparently, she could use only one wing, for she flew so wretchedly and crookedly that she almost touched the ground. Smirre not only made a high leap for her, but he also pursued her, running and jumping all the way down to the lake. But not even this time did he get anything for his trouble.

When the fourteenth goose came along, it looked very pretty because it was white. And as the great wings moved, it glistened like a light in the dark forest. When Smirre Fox saw this one, he mustered all his strength and jumped halfway up to the tree canopy. But the white one flew by unhurt like the rest.

Now it was quiet for a moment under the beeches. It looked as if the whole wild goose flock had flown past.

Suddenly Smirre remembered his prisoner and raised his eyes toward the young beech tree. And just as he might have expected — the boy had disappeared.

THE KING O' THE CATS

by JOSEPH JACOBS

Old Tom was just an ordinary cat until—

ONE winter's evening the sexton's wife was sitting by the fireside with her big black cat, Old Tom, on the other side, both half asleep and waiting for the master to come home. They waited and they waited, but still he didn't come, till at last he came rushing in, calling out, "Who's Tommy Tildrum?" in such a wild way that both his wife and his cat stared at him to know what was the matter.

"Why, what's the matter?" said his wife, "and why do you want to know who Tommy Tildrum is?"

"Oh, I've had such an adventure. I was digging away at old Mr. Fordyce's grave when I suppose I must have dropped asleep, and only woke up by hearing a cat's miaow."

"Miaow!" said Old Tom in answer.

"Yes, just like that! So I looked over the edge of the grave, and what do you think I saw?"

"Now, how can I tell?" said the sexton's wife.

"Why, nine black cats all like our friend Tom here, all with a white spot on their chestesses. And what do you think they were carrying? Why, a small coffin covered with a black velvet pall, and on the pall was a small crown all of gold, and at every third step they took they cried all together, miaow—"

"Miaow!" said Old Tom again.

"Yes, just like that!" said the sexton. "And as they came nearer and nearer to me I could see them more distinctly, because their eyes shone out with a sort of green light. Well, they all came toward me, eight of them carrying the coffin, and the biggest cat of all walking in front for all the world like—but look at our Tom, how he's looking at me. You'd think he knew all I was saying."

"Go on, go on," said his wife, "never mind Old Tom."

"Well, as I was a-saying, they came toward me slowly and solemnly, and at every third step crying all together, miaow—"

"Miaow!" said Old Tom again.

"Yes, just like that, till they came and stood right opposite Mr. Fordyce's grave, where I was, when they all stood still and looked straight at me. I did feel queer,

that I did! But look at Old Tom—he's looking at me just the way they did."

"Go on, go on," said his wife, "never mind Old Tom."

"Where was I? Oh, they all stood still looking at me, when the one that wasn't carrying the coffin came forward and, staring straight at me, said to me—yes, I told you, said to me, with a squeaky voice, 'Tell Tom Tildrum that Tim Toldrum's dead,' and that's why I asked you if you know who Tom Tildrum was, for how can I tell Tom Tildrum Tim Toldrum's dead if I don't know who Tom Tildrum is?"

"Look at Old Tom, look at Old Tom!" screamed his wife.

And well he might look, for Tom was swelling, and Tom was staring, and at last Tom shrieked out, "What—old Tim dead! then I'm king o' the Cats!" and rushed up the chimney and was nevermore seen.

THE HARE AS NURSE
TO THE BEAR CUBS

*Here is a story that Russian children loved
in the days of the Czars.*

ONCE upon a time there lived a bear, and he had a great many little bears, and, as he had no wife, he was up to his ears in work—up early in the morning, off to collect firewood—but who in the meantime was to look after the children?

So the bear came to the conclusion that this state of things simply couldn't go on—leaving little bear cubs with no one to look after them. All sorts of accidents might happen. They might scratch each other's eyes out, or mortally offend someone by their pranks. No, it was clearly necessary to find some sort of nurse.

So the bear stuffed a sack with biscuits, heaved it over his shoulder, and started off to search in high-ways and byways for someone to be a nurse to his bear cubs.

A crow was the first to turn up.

"Hello, Bear! Where are you off to?"

"I'm looking for someone to be a nurse to my bear cubs. I simply can't leave them entirely by themselves. I'm up to the ears in work, and I have to be constantly away from home."

"And what's that you've got in the sack?"

"Biscuits."

"Well, for three biscuits I'm prepared to look after your bear cubs."

"It's not the biscuits that I grudge," said the bear thoughtfully. "The question is, would you be any good as a nurse?"

"But it's quite easy. All I have to do is to say: Caw, caw! Caw, caw!" cawed the crow.

"No. That's not the sort of nurse I want," and the bear went on farther.

The next person to turn up was a vulture.

"Hello, Bear! Where are you off to?"

"I'm looking for someone to be a nurse to my bear cubs. I simply can't leave them entirely by themselves."

"And what's that you've got in the sack?"

"Biscuits."

"All right. For three biscuits I'm willing to be nurse."

"You'd find it difficult to be a nurse!" said the bear in the same thoughtful voice as before.

"There's nothing difficult about it!" And the vulture began to screech in the vulture language, enough to pierce the drums of one's ears.

But the bear wouldn't so much as discuss the matter, and went on farther.

The next person to turn up was a hare.

"Hello! Where are you going?"

"I'm looking for someone to be a nurse to my bear cubs. As you yourself know quite well, I simply can't leave them to themselves, and I'm up to the ears in work and have constantly to be away from home."

"And what have you got there in the sack?"

"Biscuits."

"If you give me the biscuits, I'll be the nurse."

"But do you know how?"

"Upon my word! Me not know? I'll stay with your cubs and I'll say to them, 'Dear little bears, my little crooked-pawed bearikins, sit still, don't growl, don't stamp about, Daddy's coming home from the wood with honey and raspberries. Oh! Such lots of sugary honeycombs and sweet raspberries!' I'll talk to them, I'll stroke them down their little backs, and down their little bellies, their soft little bellies, and I'll say to them,

'Oh you little bears! Oh you funny crooked-pawed little bears!'"

The bear drank in his words and was touched to the heart.

"Well that's a bargain. You'll make a splendid nurse."

"Of course I will!" and the hare twitched his ears. "Now then, let's see what's in the sack."

The bear opened the sack, and the hare poked in his little nose, sniffed the biscuits all over, and was well

satisfied with the results of his investigation.

"I close with the bargain," he said.

The bear heaved the sack—the hare's wages—onto his shoulders and led the hare back to his cave and his bear cubs.

"Bear cubs, here's a nurse for you. And you've got to mind him!"

And the hare snuggled down into the bear's cave, where he became a fine nurse for all the little bears.

HOW THE COYOTE MADE MAN

Some people of long ago believed that the world was made by animals. The Miwok Indians of North America believed it was made by the little prairie wolf called a coyote. And they believed that when the coyote finished making the world, he made the animals, and when he had made the animals, he made the first man.

AFTER the coyote had finished making the world and the animals, he called a meeting of animals to talk about making a man. They sat down in an open space in the forest, all in a circle, with the lion at the head. On the lion's right sat the grizzly bear. Next to the grizzly bear was the cinnamon bear. And so it went around the circle, each animal seated according to his size and fierceness until it ended with the little mouse, who sat at the lion's left.

The lion was the first to speak, and he said he would like to see a man made with a mighty voice, so that he could frighten all the animals. Then the lion would cover man all over with hair, and put terrible teeth in his jaws and strong claws on his feet.

Next it was the grizzly bear's turn to speak. He said it was silly to have a voice like the lion's, because it was so loud it frightened away the animals man wanted to capture. The old grizzly said a man ought to be very strong, and move about silently but very swiftly if he had to, and should be able to grab his prey without making a noise.

Then the big buck deer spoke. He said a man would look very foolish unless he had a magnificent pair of

antlers on his head to fight with. He agreed with the bear that it was ridiculous to roar so loudly. If he were making a man, he would pay less attention to his voice than he would to his ears and eyes. He would give him ears like a spider's web, and eyes like fire.

The mountain sheep said he never could see what sense there was in having antlers that branched every way. They were always getting caught in the bushes. If the man had nicely rolled-up horns, they would be like a stone on each side of his head, and that would make his head heavy so that he could butt much harder.

When it came to the coyote's turn to speak, he said he had just been listening to the stupidest speeches he had ever heard. He said he could hardly stay awake listening to such a pack of noodles and nincompoops. Why, every one of the animals wanted to make a man exactly like himself! It would be just as sensible to take one of their own cubs and call it a man.

The coyote then went on to say that he knew he was not the best animal that could be made, and he could make one better than himself or any other animal. Of course, the man would have to be like himself in having four legs, five fingers, and all that sort of thing. And he might have a voice like the lion's, only he did not have to roar all the time with it.

There the coyote stopped to clear his throat and look around the circle to see how the other animals were taking his speech. They were all frowning.

The coyote hurried on. The grizzly bear also had some good points, he said. One of them was the shape of his feet, which made it possible for him to stand on two legs. The coyote believed a man should have feet very much like a grizzly bear's.

The grizzly was lucky, said the coyote, that he had no tail. He knew from his own experience that a tail was good for nothing except a nest for fleas. Therefore, he would make a man without a tail.

By this time the animals were frowning harder than ever, so the coyote hurried on again. He said the buck's eyes and ears were pretty good, and he would propose giving them to the man.

Just then the fish began to glare at the coyote and opened his mouth to speak. So the coyote hurried on. He said he envied the nakedness of the fish, because hair was so dreadfully warm in the summer. Therefore, he would make a man without hair. He would give him claws like the eagle's, so that he could hold things in them. And then he said that all the animals must admit that there was no one so clever and tricky as himself, and so he would like to give the man that part of himself, too.

When the coyote had finished speaking, the beaver said he had never heard such nonsense and twaddle in his life. No tail, indeed! He would make a man with a broad, flat tail so he could haul mud and sand on it.

The owl said all the animals seemed to have lost their senses. None of them wanted to give the man wings. He could not see what use anything on earth could be to a man if he had no wings.

The mole said it was absolutely crazy to talk about wings. If a man had wings, he was sure to bump his head against the sky. Besides, if he had both wings and eyes, he would get his eyes burned out by flying too near the sun. Without eyes, he could burrow in the cool, soft earth and be happy.

Last of all the little mouse squeaked out that he would make a man with eyes, of course, so that he could see what he was eating. As for burrowing in the ground, what person in his senses would want to do such a thing?

So the animals disagreed among themselves, and the meeting broke up in a fight. The coyote flew at the beaver and nipped a piece out of his tail. The owl jumped on top of the coyote's head and began to pull his hair out. There was a high old time! Then every animal set to work to make a man that was like himself out of a lump of earth. But the coyote stole off to one side and began to make a man such as he had described.

It was so late when they began to work that night came before they had finished. They all lay down and fell asleep. But the clever coyote stayed awake and worked hard on his model all night. Then, while the other animals were still asleep, he threw water on all their models, and spoiled them.

Early in the morning the coyote finished his model of a man and gave it life. And that is how man was made by the coyote.

NOT QUITE MARTIN

by LEON WILSON

The huckleberries were ripe on Cumberland Mountain down in Tennessee, and Cody Capshaw decided that just for once he was going to eat all he wanted of the black, juicy fruit. He guessed it would take a long time to eat enough to satisfy him, so he chose the longest day in summer for his feast. He'd counted on getting home before night, but the huckle bushes went on and on over the mountain, and by the time Cody was satisfied, all outdoors was dark as a pocket.

NOW if you were alone in the woods and it was pitch-black dark, maybe you would be a little frightened. Cody Capshaw wasn't, though. He knew all about the woods in these Kentucky mountains, and being alone in the dark didn't worry him a bit. Of course he would have preferred being home with Milt and Callie and Omalia, but since this was out, he didn't intend to waste time wishing he was some place he couldn't be.

What he had to do was decide how and where to spend the night.

He wasn't sleepy yet because it wasn't bedtime, and he wasn't cold because it was midsummer, and he wasn't hungry because he was cram-jam full of his favorite food. All these things he wasn't. The main thing he was, was tired of bumping into trees.

Now just as the last speck of daylight had vanished, Cody had sighted a little log cabin in which no one lived.

This is how he knew no one lived in it —

First thing: no light in the window.

Second thing: no smoke looping out of the chimney.

Third thing: no one moving around inside the cabin. Cody found this out by putting his ear to a crack in the logs and listening.

He couldn't hear a sound.

"Here's my home for tonight," says Cody to himself, mighty proud of his cleverness, and he climbs the steps to the door, and just to make absolutely completely sure no one is inside, he knocks loudly.

No answer.

(He would have been mighty surprised, of course, if there *had* been an answer!)

So he pushes the door open and takes a look inside. But you can bet he doesn't see much, for it's as dark in there as the inside of a cow.

109

He lights one of his matches and looks again. And sees? — nothing. Or almost nothing. Just an old empty cabin. Not a chair or a table in it; not a lamp, a dish, or a bed. A few old sticks lying around on the floor to make a fire with, and that's all.

So in pops Cody, mighty pleased with himself, and shuts the door and scrammishes together some wood and makes himself a fire in the fireplace.

"Why shucks," he says to himself, "this is almost as good as being home. The only thing I lack here that I would have at home (besides a dish of the huckleberry pie my mother was baking) is someone to talk to. Too bad I hit my dog Daybreak with that stick. I should have let him come along — I'd have some company now."

And now, listen:

The very minute he thinks about company, there comes a tap-tap-tap on the cabin door.

Very soft. So soft Cody hardly hears it. So soft Cody believes he has gone to sleep and he's dreaming that he heard it.

And now it comes again. A little louder this time. About like this: TAP-TAP-TAP.

This time Cody knows he's really hearing something. "Who in the world can be out there?" he asks himself. "Can't be anyone coming to see me, for who knows I'm here? Nobody!" He scratches his head to help himself think. "Maybe," he decides, "it's someone come to visit whoever it is that doesn't live here any more."

And now on the door there comes a good loud TAP-TAP-TAPPETY-TAP.

(Whoever's out there, he's getting tired of waiting. He's wanting an answer.)

"Open the door and come in, sir," Cody says politely. "Whoever you are, come in and enjoy my good fire with me."

Cody hears the door begin to open. He turns his head and peeks over his shoulder. And sees —

Not a man —

Not a woman —

Not a boy —

And no, not even a girl —

He sees a cat. A gray stripy cat with a long stripy tail.

The instant Cody sees it he knows it is no ordinary cat. For one thing, its yellow eyes are bigger and brighter and yellower by a good deal than an ordinary cat's are. For another thing, this cat's whiskers are longer and its gray stripy tail is much longer than even Midnight's, and Midnight's is pretty long.

I haven't told you yet how surprised Cody is, but you can imagine!

He's so surprised, in fact, seeing a cat walk in when he expected to see a man, that he now says to the cat the very thing he had planned to say to the man.

"Good evening, sir," he says.

And the little cat switches his long stripy tail and looks Cody over with his big, bright, yellow eyes and replies as polite as you please:

"Good evening to you, sir."

Cody is really surprised this time! He has seen clever cats before. Midnight, for instance. If no one is around to help Midnight, she will push a door open when she wants in or pull it open when she wants out. But clever as Midnight is, she doesn't *talk!* Cody guesses mighty few cats are clever enough to talk, and he decides to keep an eye on this one and see what clever thing it will do next.

But the cat doesn't do much more. It pushes the door shut, but then that's no great feat for even an ordinary cat. Then it strolls to the hearthstone and plumps down where it's warm from the fire and tucks its paws under its chest, the way a cat will. And it curls its long stripy tail around itself, and that's all.

Or just about all. One thing more: it turns its big bright eyes on Cody and gives him one of those long-lasting looks cats are so good at.

Cody grins at the little critter, hoping it will feel at home and talk some more, but the cat says not another word. It yawns one of those gaping yawns cats go in for and then it returns to watching Cody's fire. And this time, this is really all it does.

"Pretty nice fire, isn't it?" Cody remarks. He's out to make the little thing talk.

Does the cat reply? It does not! Does the cat even look at Cody again? It does not! It goes on watching the fire for all the world as if it hadn't heard Cody speak.

Cody shakes his head. "What a crying shame!" he says to himself. He's pretty sure he's never going to meet another cat clever enough to talk. Too bad this one won't open up so he can find out what cats think about.

And now on the cabin door there comes a rap-rap-rap. Not loud, but louder than the cat's tap-tap-tap. About like this: RAP-RAP-RAP.

"Well!" says Cody to himself. "Who is it this time? Someone looking for the man who doesn't live here any more, or another cat?"

Cody thinks it would be dandy if another talking cat came in. Might be just what this fellow on the hearthstone needs to get him going. Then while the two cats discussed cat matters together, he could sit here and listen and learn.

RAPPETY-RAP-RAP-RAP! Good and loud this time — and Cody realizes that with all his wondering who it is, he's been keeping the rapper waiting. He pops his mouth open to say "Come in, whoever you are," but before he has a chance to say it, the cat on the hearthstone cries out:

"You're wasting your time rapping — open and enter!"

Before Cody can get over his surprise at this, he has to peek over his shoulder again, for the door is opening.

A man this time?

No.

Another cat, then?

No, not another cat.

A big old smiling possum!

Chances are you've never seen a possum. If you haven't, you've missed something. Possums' eyes are small, almost as small as apple seeds, and their mouths are famous for the very long, thin, white teeth in them, and possums are famous too for their tails, which are not only long and thin but almost completely hairless.

Cody has seen possums before this, of course, for there are lots of them on Cumberland Mountain, but in all his life he has never seen such a possumy-looking possum as this one coming in the door. Never has he seen such very long, sharp teeth or such a completely sickly smile.

And what does this most possumy-looking possum do? Nothing very much. It shuts the door and then comes creeping across the floor in that slow-going, take-it-easy way possums have, and slides in beside the cat. Then it looks up at Cody with its eyes that are like two shiny apple seeds, and of course it continues to smile its half-happy, half-unhappy bellyache smile. And now it turns to the cat and asks in a take-it-easy possum sort of drawl:

"How soon?" and at the same time it jerks its head toward Cody so the cat will know what it's talking about.

The cat glances up at Cody with his bright golden eyes and says to the possum, as plain as you please:

"We can't do nothin' till Martin comes."

This seems to satisfy the possum. Smiling its bellyache smile, it says not another word and commences watching the fire.

Cody politely waits for the cat and the possum to say something more, even though he has a question troubling him. "Excuse me, please," he says finally.

The cat and the possum look up to find out what's on Cody's mind.

"I heard you mention Martin," Cody says. "Who is Martin, and about how soon do you reckon he'll be coming along?"

The cat looks at the possum but says nothing. The possum looks at the cat and says nothing.

So all Cody can do is wonder about Martin.

And now, on the door: Scrape-scrape-scrape.

This time Cody finds he isn't much interested in saying "Come in, whoever you are." Maybe it's Martin, and maybe he doesn't care to see Martin coming in, making himself at home. The more Cody thinks it may be Martin, the more he wants to think no one is outside at all, so he tries his level best to believe that the wind is blowing a tree branch against the door. Of course the scraping noise is a bit loud, especially when there isn't a breath of wind stirring — but Cody thinks there's no harm in trying.

Now here it comes again, much louder:

SCRAPE-SCRAPE-SCRAPE.

(It certainly isn't a tree branch!)

"Kick it open and join us!" the possum calls out in a loud voice, and the little cat cries out:

"We're waiting for you!"

This time, as the door opens, Cody takes his time peeking around. He isn't by any means certain he wants to see who is coming in.

And who is? Another cat? Another possum? Martin? Not quite.

When Cody gets his eyes around, he sees a sleek red fox with high pointed ears, a long pointed nose, shiny at the tip, and eyes as glittery as two polished black marbles. And a tail so bushy and long that it's almost the size of the fox.

And what does he do, this fox who is bigger than the possum who in turn is bigger than the little cat? Well, he doesn't do anything, unless you want to call shutting the door something.

He steps quieter than a whisper across to the hearthstone and glides in beside the possum. Then he swings his rusty red head Cody's way and slowly winks one of his glittery black eyes for all the world as if he and Cody are sharing some deep secret.

Then he turns to the possum and the cat and in his supersleek, soft foxy voice, he asks:

"How soon?"

And the cat and the possum answer, "We can't do nothin' till Martin comes."

"Oh," says the fox, and once again he looks up at Cody and slyly winks one eye.

And while the fox winks, the possum smiles his bellyache smile, and the little cat stares at Cody with his bright

yellow eyes that every minute seem to grow a little bigger.

And all the time the animals are watching Cody, Cody is thinking. He's thinking so hard about something good to eat that he can almost taste it.

Strangely enough, it isn't huckleberries. It's an enormous plate of yellow cornbread fixed up with butter and bee honey. And right beside the steaming hot cornbread is a dish piled high with — have you guessed? — leather breeches. And just beyond the breeches sits a glass of ice-cold buttermilk at least ten inches tall.

What a slam-gorgeous supper, Cody thinks — my, if only I was home this minute with my ears pinned back, eating such a supper, I wouldn't be here in this crowded old cabin that's getting more crowded every minute. Boy, what I wouldn't give for a mess of cornbread!

And right in the middle of Cody's cornbread thinking:
CRACKETY-BANG!

The door again, and this time it doesn't begin to sound like a branch scraping in the wind. All it sounds like is someone in a burning hurry to enter.

"Kick it open and roll in!" cries the fox.

"Waitin' for you!" cries the possum.

"Me too!" cries the cat.

When Cody peeks over his shoulder this time, he sees a panther!

(Now if you've never seen a panther, an easy way to imagine what this one looked like is to think how that little cat beyond the possum would look if it wasn't little but gigantic.)

What a whopper of a panther this one coming in the door is! His ears are as big as Easter baskets. His eyes are as bright as two flashlights. His whiskers stick out like knitting needles. His tail is so long Cody wonders if it's ever going to end. (It does end, finally, but not for a long time.)

And what does the panther do? Nothing much. He shuts the door, of course — but then they all shut the door — and he stalks to the hearthstone and moves in beside the fox.

Then he turns his flashlight eyes on Cody and he looks the boy up, looks him down, looks him back, looks him forth, and after he's looked at Cody all these ways, he turns to the fox and the possum and the cat and, in a gigantic, panthery voice, he says just one word:

"When?"

And the cat and the possum and the fox all reply at once:

"We can't do nothin' till Martin comes."

Now all the time this is going on, something else has been happening that I haven't had a chance to mention: Cody's fine fire has been burning lower and lower the way any fire will when you fail to feed it. By now, the fire is so low and the cabin is so dark that when Cody looks at his four visitors, this is just about all he can see:

The stary yellow eyes of the little cat —

The shiny apple-seed eyes of the smiling possum —

The glittery marble eyes of the fox (one of them slowly winking from time to time) —

And the flashlight eyes of the panther —

And all these eyes are looking straight at Cody!

So Cody scrammishes around in a hurry and builds up his fire. He wants to see more than just eyes. Yes sir, as long as he has to sit here, he wants a good view of the folks he's sitting with.

And now at the door there is a new noise — not a tap, not a rap, not a scrape, not a CRACKETY-BANG but one tremendous — CRASH! as the door flies back and in springs the biggest old black bear Cody has ever seen. He's two sizes bigger than the biggest bear Cody has ever even dreamed of seeing, and he's three shades blacker, and his black shiny eyes look as big as doorknobs.

And what does he do, this bear of all bears? One thing he doesn't do: he doesn't shut the door. Hasn't time. Too big a hurry.

One spring and he's on the hearthstone beside the panther, and he's looking Cody over with his doorknob eyes, but not for long, because he has to find out something in a hurry — right now! He turns to quiz the panther, the fox, the possum, and the cat, but before he can say anything, they all reply at once:

"We can't do nothin' till Martin comes!"

"Thanks for telling me," says the bear in a booming, bear sort of voice and he turns to look at Cody again.

But now, what's this? Where is Cody?

The animals look around the cabin quickly, thinking maybe he has run away.

But Cody hasn't gone anywhere — not yet. He's standing in the middle of the cabin looking down at his feet, and anyone can see that something about his feet is worrying him.

As the animals watch, Cody begins stamping. One foot and then the other. He makes quite a bit of noise with them.

The animals look at one another in amazement. "What's the big idea?" they seem to be saying. "Why this stamp-

ing? Why isn't this boy Cody sitting here enjoying this good fire with us while we wait for Martin?"

And perhaps you are wondering.

I'll tell you:

Back when the panther came stalking in, Cody began to feel an itchy sensation in his feet that wouldn't go away. In fact, the longer he sat on the hearthstone doing nothing to get rid of the sensation, the itchier it became. By the time the bear burst in, Cody's feet were itching him so bad he couldn't sit still another second.

That's why he's stamping now in the middle of the cabin.

"Itch in my feet," he informs the bewildered animals. He can tell from the way they look at him that they don't believe a word of it. The yellow eyes of the little cat and the possum's apple seeds and the fox's glittery marbles and the panther's flashlights and the bear's doorknobs are all as full of disbelief as they can be.

"Young Mr. Cody seems not to care for our company," the animals appear to be saying.

Cody is sorry they don't believe him, but he doesn't see what he can do about it. After all, he's telling them the truth — it's their tough luck if they won't believe him.

"Stamping helps some," he goes on, "but not enough. I believe I've got to walk some. Walk fast. This little old cabin isn't half big enough for the walking I've got to do. I'd be hitting the walls six times a minute, trying to do my walking in here."

All the time Cody is explaining this, he's backing slowly to the door, and now he stands with one of his itchy feet already outside on the steps, waiting to go.

"Friends," he says — and his feet are so impatient he can hardly stand still long enough to say this one more thing he wants to say — "friends," he says quietly and politely, "when Martin gets here, tell him I was here, please, and tell him I waited for him as long as I could, but I couldn't wait one minute more."

And saying this, Cody commences his fast walk away from the cabin, and do you know? — the minute he looks back and sees that the cat and the possum and the fox and the panther and the bear aren't following him, his feet practically entirely stop itching!

Well, that's the adventure Cody had the day he ate more huckleberries than he had ever eaten before.

The sun was coming up as he started his swift departure from that cabin, so it wasn't a great time before he was home again, eating breakfast with Milt and Callie and Omalia. Between bites of pie (for Cody's breakfast was a piece of the huckle pie he had missed out on the night before), Cody told his story exactly as I have told it: how he met the cat, the possum, the fox, the panther, the bear, and almost, but not quite, Martin. The minute he finished, Omalia, who had been listening pop-eyed to every word, exclaimed:

"Fiddle faddle! You made it up to give us a thrill."

"Made it up!" Cody said indignantly.

"Possums don't talk," Omalia said, "and neither do cats or panthers or foxes or bears."

"This possum talked," Cody said, "and so did the rest of them. Shucks, they talked all kinds of stuff."

Omalia shook her head and looked exceedingly wise for a little girl of seven. "I suspect," she said sternly, "you went in that cabin and fell asleep and dreamed every bit of it."

"Dreamed it?" Cody cried. "You wouldn't have thought it was a dream if you'd been there!"

Omalia went right on as if she hadn't heard Cody. "In fact," she said, addressing her mother and father, "I've made up my mind it was a dream. Cody must have eaten some green huckleberries and they didn't sit right."

"Dream!" Cody muttered, spooning up the pie juice on his plate. "Green huckleberries!" Suddenly his face puckered up with thought.

"What's the matter, Cody?" his mother asked. She

127

feared Cody might not be feeling well, having been up so late the night before.

"Nothing's the matter," Cody said. "I'm thinking."

"Thinking what?" Milt asked, for he could see that Cody was pretty worried.

"He's thinking how glad he is we saved him this little ol' slab of pie," Omalia suggested.

"I'm thinking," Cody said slowly, "maybe my feet shouldn't have gotten itchy just when they did. Golly, the very next one might have been Martin himself. Now I'll always wonder who Martin was and never know."

"Dreams like that," Omalia said in her most grown-up tone, "always disappoint you when you wake up."

No sooner had she said this than there came a strange thumping noise at the front door. Omalia's heart almost jumped out of her mouth! Quickly she reached for the cream pitcher so Cody wouldn't see how startled she was.

But Cody was watching the door, not his sister. The door was opening, slowly, mysteriously. Cody felt the hair on the back of his neck begin to creep. He held his breath.

And Omalia forgot completely about the cream and held her breath!

And the door swung wide and in walked —

Yes, a cat — but this time the cat was a normal-looking, non-talking cat with regulation-size eyes. Just Midnight looking for breakfast.

Cody sighed in relief. Then he looked at his mother and father and Omalia. "Dream or not," he said, grinning, "that's exactly the way it started!"

WELL DONE AND ILL PAID

*In most folk tales, the fox is a sly fellow who well deserves
his punishment. In this story from Norway he does a good deed
and is tricked himself.*

ONCE upon a time there was a man who had to drive
his sledge to the forest for wood. And he met a bear.

"Give me your horse," said the bear, "or I'll eat all
your sheep by summer."

"Heaven help me!" said the man. "There's not a stick of firewood in the house. You must let me drive home a load of wood or we will freeze to death. I'll bring the horse to you tomorrow morning."

The bear said that would be all right, but he added a warning. "If you don't come back," he said, "remember that I'm going to eat up your sheep."

So the man got the wood on the sledge and rattled homeward, but he wasn't at all pleased with the bargain, as you can imagine.

When he was nearly home he met a fox, and the fox asked, "What's the matter? What makes you look so worried?"

"Oh, if you want to know," said the man, "I met a bear up yonder in the woods, and I had to promise him to bring Dobbin back tomorrow. If that bear doesn't get Dobbin, he'll eat all my sheep by summer."

"Oh, if it's nothing worse than that!" said the fox. "If you'll give me your fattest sheep, I'll soon set you free."

The man gave his word, and swore he would keep it, too.

"Well, when you come with Dobbin for the bear tomorrow," said the fox, "I'll make a clatter up in that heap of stones yonder. When the bear asks what that noise is, you must say it is Peter the Hunter, who is the best shot in the world. And after that you must help yourself."

The next day the man set off for the woods with old Dobbin, and when he met the bear, something began to make a clatter up in the heap of stones.

"Hist! What's that?" asked the bear.

"Oh, that's Peter the Hunter, to be sure," said the man. "He's the best shot in the world. I know him by his voice."

"Have you seen any bears around here, my friend?" shouted a voice from the heap of stones.

"Say no!" said the bear.

"No, I haven't seen any," said the man.

"What's that, then, standing alongside your sledge?" bawled out the voice from the woods.

"Say it's an old tree stump," said the bear.

"Oh, it's only an old tree stump," said the man.

"In our country, we take old tree stumps and roll them on our sledges," bawled out the voice. "If you can't do it yourself, I'll come and help you."

"Say you can help yourself, and roll me up on the sledge," said the bear.

"No, thank you, I can help myself well enough," said the man, and rolled the bear onto the sledge.

"In our country we always bind a tree stump fast on our sledges," bawled out the voice. "Shall I come and help you?"

"Say you can help yourself, and bind me fast, do," said the bear.

"No, thanks, I can help myself well enough," said the man, and he bound the bear fast with all the ropes he had, so that in the end the bear couldn't move a paw.

"In our part of the world we always drive our ax
into a tree stump once we have bound it to our sledge,"
bawled the voice. "Then we can guide it better going
down the slopes."

"Pretend to drive your ax into me, do now," said the
bear.

Then the man took up his ax and at one blow split
the bear's skull.

The fox came out of the woods, and he and the man
were the best of friends. But when they came near the
man's farm the fox said: "I don't think I'll go any farther
with you because I don't like your dogs. I'll just wait
here, and you can bring the sheep to me. And be sure
you pick out a nice fat one."

The man said he would be sure to do that, and thanked the fox very much indeed for his help. So he drove home with the bear to make a fur coat out of him, and was very happy at the bargain he had made.

When the man had put Dobbin in his stall, he started for the sheep pen.

"Where are you going now?" asked his wife.

"Oh," said the man, "I am only going to the sheep pen. I have to find a fat sheep for that smart fox who saved our Dobbin."

"Sheep indeed!" said the wife. "Never a one shall that thief of a fox get! Haven't we got Dobbin safe, and the bear into the bargain? As for the fox, I'll bet he's stolen more of our geese than the sheep is worth. And even if he hasn't stolen them, he will. No, don't you dare take one of the sheep to the fox! Take two of your fastest hounds in a bag, and slip them loose after him. Then perhaps we will be rid of this robbing fox."

Well, the man thought that was pretty good advice. He took two fast red hounds, put them into a bag, and set off with them.

"Have you brought the sheep?" asked the fox.

"Yes, come and take it," said the man as he untied the sack and let loose the hounds.

"Huf!" said the fox, and gave a great leap. "It is true what I have heard, 'Well done is often ill paid.' And now I know, too, the truth of another saying, 'Your worst foes are often your friends.'"

That was what the fox said as he ran off with the two hounds at his heels.

THE FOOLISH PEACOCK

Do you wish you had a high-sounding name? Here is what happened to the peacock when he decided to change his name.

ONCE there was a peacock who was so proud of his beautiful tail that he did nothing all day long but strut around spreading it and screeching to call attention to himself. When the farmer called, "Pee-wee, pee-wee, pee-wee," he looked the other way and pretended he didn't hear.

"You're missing a lot of good things," said the hen. "When the farmer calls 'Pee-wee, pee-wee, pee-wee,' or 'Chick-chick-chick,' he is scattering corn for us to eat."

137

"Pee-wee isn't my name," said the peacock haughtily. And he spread his tail and stuck out his neck and screeched, "My name is Beautiful-is-his-tail-as-the-sun-coming-over-the-mountain-in-the-mists-of-the-morning. Get it? Now don't you ever call me anything else or I'll peck your eyes out."

"I'll never call you anything else," promised the hen, who was afraid of the peacock's fierce beak, "never, never, never!"

Just then a fox came out of the woods and grabbed the peacock and started to drag him away. "Help! Help!" screamed the peacock. "Run to the cat and tell her to rescue me from the fox!"

So the hen ran to the cat and said, "Hurry! Hurry! The fox has carried off Beautiful-is-his-tail-as-the-sun-coming-over-the-mountain-in-the-mists-of-the-morning."

"Who?" asked the cat. "Whoever is Beautiful-is-his-tail-as-the-sun-coming-over-the-mountain-in-the-mists-of-the-morning?"

"It is the peacock," said the hen. "Oh, hurry, hurry, hurry! It is his new name, and you are not to call him by any other."

"Rubbish," said the cat, bounding off the porch.
"Anyhow, I'm too small to catch a fox. I'll have to
find the dog."

"But mind you call the peacock by his new name,"
squawked the hen. "If you don't, he will peck your eyes
out."

"I wouldn't care for that," said the cat, and away she
went to find the dog.

The dog was asleep in the sun, and when he heard the
cat coming he jumped up and bristled the hair on his
neck.

"Now, now!" said the cat. "This is no time to chase
me. Beautiful-is-his-tail-as-the-sun-coming-over-the-
mountain-in-the-mists-of-the-morning has been carried
away by the fox."

"And who is Beautiful-is-his-tail-as-the-sun-coming-
over-the-mountain-in-the-mists-of-the-morning?" demanded the dog. "I never heard such a name."

"It is the new name the peacock has given himself,"

said the cat. "If you call him by any other, he will peck your eyes out."

"Well," said the dog, "I don't want my eyes pecked out, but by the same token, I don't want to waste my time rescuing a bird with such a long name. I'll go and find the farmer."

And away he ran to the farmer, who was mowing the hay. "Master! Master!" he barked. "Beautiful-is-his-tail-as-the-sun-coming-over-the-mountain-in-the-mists-of-the-morning has been carried away by the fox."

"What did you say?" asked the farmer, who was a little deaf. "Who's been carried away by the fox?"

"Beautiful-is-his-tail-as-the-sun-coming-over-the-mountain-in-the-mists-of-the-morning," repeated the dog.

"I get it," said the farmer, shaking his head. "I thought 'twas a whole family you were talking about. But who *is* Beautiful-is-his-tail-as-the-sun-coming-over-the-mountain-in-the-mists-of-the-morning?"

"It's the peacock," said the dog. "He's given himself a new name. And don't you call him by any other, or he'll peck your eyes out."

"I'll wring his neck!" shouted the farmer, and away he ran to rescue the peacock.

By the time the farmer reached the fox's den, the fox had eaten the peacock, feathers and all. When the hen heard the news she said, "If he'd been satisfied to answer to Pee-wee, he'd still be strutting around the yard. When it's my turn to be rescued, just call me Chick."

"Call me Puss," purred the cat, gathering in her paws for a nap.

"Call me Spot," said the dog, and went off to look for his dinner.

THE TAR BABY

by DORA LEE NEWMAN

This story is so old that nobody really knows where it began. It is told in Europe, India, Africa, South America, and among the North American Indians. But it is not always exactly the same story. Sometimes the tar baby is a doll made of tree gum, and sometimes the rabbit is a man. The tar baby story that has long been popular in the United States was probably brought to America by African slaves. Joel Chandler Harris told it in Negro dialect in his Uncle Remus stories.

ONCE upon a time there was no water. The ponds went dry, and the brooks went dry, and the rivers went dry. There was no water anywhere. So all the animals in the forest met together to see what they could do about it. The lion and the bear and the wolf, the fox and the giraffe and the monkey, the elephant, and even the rabbit were at the meeting. And they all tried to think of some way to get water.

At last the animals decided to dig a well. Everybody said he would help—everybody except the rabbit, who was always a lazy fellow. He said he was too tired to dig.

Then all the animals said, "Very well, Mr. Rabbit, if you won't help us dig this well, you shan't have one drop of water to drink."

But the rabbit just laughed and said, as smart as you please, "Never mind, you dig the well, and I'll get a drink all right."

The animals worked very hard, all except the rabbit. Soon they had the well so deep that they struck water.

Then they all had a drink, and went away to their homes in the forest.

The very next morning they came for another drink, and what should they find but the rabbit's footprints in the mud at the edge of the well. They knew he had come in the night and stolen some water. So they all began to think how they could keep that lazy rabbit from getting another drink. They talked and talked and talked, and after a while they decided that someone must watch the well. But when it came right down to it, nobody wanted to stay up that late.

At last the bear said, "I'll watch the well the first night. You just go to bed, and I'll show little old Mr. Rabbit that he won't get any water while I'm around."

Then all the animals went home to bed, and the bear sat down by the well.

By-and-by the rabbit came out of the thicket on the hillside. When he saw the bear guarding the well he didn't know what to do. Then he sat down and began to sing:

"*Cha ra ra, will you, will you, can you?*
Cha ra ra, will you, will you, can you?"

Before long the old bear lifted up his head and looked around. "Where's all that pretty music coming from?" he said.

The rabbit kept right on singing:

"*Cha ra ra, will you, will you, can you?*
Cha ra ra, will you, will you, can you?"

This time the bear got up on his hind feet. The rabbit kept on singing:

"Cha ra ra, will you, will you, can you?
Cha ra ra, will you, will you, can you?"

Then the bear began to dance, and after a while he danced so far away that the rabbit wasn't afraid any longer. He climbed down into the well and got a drink and ran away into the thicket.

When the animals came the next morning and found the rabbit's footprints in the mud, they made all kinds of fun of old Mr. Bear. They said, "Mr. Bear, you are a fine person to watch a well. Why, even Mr. Rabbit can fool you."

But the bear said, "The rabbit had nothing to do with it. I was sitting here wide-awake when suddenly the most beautiful music came right down out of the sky. At least I think it came down out of the sky, for when I went to look for it, I could not find it. It must have been while I was gone that Mr. Rabbit stole the water."

"Anyway," said the other animals, "we can't trust you any more. Mr. Monkey, you had better watch the well tonight, and mind you, you'd better be careful, or old Mr. Rabbit will fool you."

"I'd like to see him do it," said the monkey. "Just let him try."

So the animals set the monkey to watch the well.

In a little while it grew dark, and all the stars came out. Then the rabbit slipped out of the thicket and peeped

over in the direction of the well. When he saw the monkey, he sat down on the hillside and began to sing:

> "*Cha ra ra, will you, will you, can you?*
> *Cha ra ra, will you, will you, can you?*"

The monkey peered down into the well. "It isn't the water," said he.

The rabbit kept on singing:

> "*Cha ra ra, will you, will you, can you?*
> *Cha ra ra, will you, will you, can you?*"

This time the monkey looked into the sky. "It isn't the stars," said he.

The rabbit kept on singing.

This time the monkey looked toward the forest. "It must be the leaves," said he. "Anyway, such fine music must not go to waste."

With that the monkey began to dance, and after a while he danced so far away that the rabbit wasn't afraid of him any longer. The rabbit climbed down into the well and got a drink and ran off into the thicket.

Well, the next morning, when all the animals came down and found the footprints again, you should have heard them talk to that monkey. They said, "Mr. Monkey, you are no better than Mr. Bear. Neither of you is any good. You can't catch a rabbit."

The monkey answered, "It wasn't old Mr. Rabbit's fault at all that I left the well. He had nothing to do with it. All at once the most beautiful music you ever heard came out of the woods, and I went to see who was making it."

When the animals were through laughing at the monkey, they tried to get someone else to watch the well that night. No one would do it. So they thought and thought about what they would do next. Finally the fox said, "I'll tell you what let's do; let's make a tar baby and set him to watch the well."

"Let's do!" said all the other animals together.

So they worked the whole day long building a tar baby, and then they set him to watch the well.

That night the rabbit crept out of the thicket, and there he saw the tar baby. So he sat down on the hillside and began to sing:

"Cha ra ra, will you, will you, can you?
Cha ra ra, will you, will you, can you?"

But the tar baby never heard a word.
The rabbit came a little closer and sang:

"Cha ra ra, will you, will you, can you?
Cha ra ra, will you, will you, can you?"

The tar baby never spoke.
The rabbit came a little closer still and sang:

"Cha ra ra, will you, will you, can you?
Cha ra ra, will you, will you, can you?"

The tar baby never spoke a word.

Now the rabbit came right up close to the tar baby. "Look here," he said, "you get out of my way and let me down into the well."

The tar baby never moved.

"If you don't get out of my way, I'll hit you with my fist," said the rabbit.

The tar baby never moved a finger.

Then the rabbit raised his fist and struck the tar baby as hard as he could, and his right fist stuck tight in the tar. "Now you let go of me or I'll hit you with my other fist," said the rabbit.

The tar baby never budged.

Then the rabbit struck him with his left fist, and his left fist stuck tight in the tar. "Now you let go of my fists or I'll kick you with my foot," said the rabbit.

The tar baby never moved an inch.

Then the rabbit kicked him with his right foot, and his right foot stuck tight in the tar. "Now you let go of my foot or I'll kick you with my other foot," said the rabbit.

The tar baby never stirred.

Then the rabbit kicked him with his left foot, and his left foot stuck tight in the tar. "Now you let me go or I'll butt you with my head," said the rabbit. And he butted him with his head, and there Mr. Rabbit was; and there the other animals found him the next morning.

Well, you should have heard those animals laugh. "Oh, ho, Mr. Rabbit," they said. "Now we'll see whether you steal any more of our water or not. We're going to

lay you across the log and cut your head off."

"Oh, please do," said the rabbit. "I've always wanted to have my head cut off."

"Then we won't do it," said the other animals. "We are not going to do what you want us to do. We are going to shoot you."

"That's better," said the rabbit. "If I had stopped to think, I'd have asked you to do that in the first place. Please shoot me."

"No, we won't shoot you," said the other animals. And they thought and thought a long time to find something the rabbit wouldn't like.

"I'll tell you what we'll do," said the bear. "We'll put you into a cupboard and let you eat and eat and eat until you are as fat as butter, and then we'll throw you up into the air and let you come down and burst."

"Oh, please don't!" begged the rabbit, "I never wanted that to happen to me. Just do anything else, but please don't burst me."

"Then that's exactly what we'll do," said all the other animals together.

So they put the rabbit into the cupboard and they fed him pie and cake and sugar, everything that was good. And by-and-by the rabbit got just as fat as butter. Then they took him out on the hillside, and the lion took a paw, and the fox took a paw, and the bear took a paw, and the monkey took a paw, and they swung him back and forth, saying, "One for the money, two for the show, three to make ready, and four to Go!"

And up they tossed him into the air!

Now the rabbit was so fat that when he came down, he bounced. He bounced two feet, three feet up into the air again. Then he came down and landed on all fours and sang:

"*Yipp! My name's Peter Rabbit!*
Catch me if you can!"

And off he ran into the thicket.

THE CRAB AND THE CRANE

In the myths of ancient Egypt the crab was a monster called the makara, who carried the goddess of the Nile on his back. But to many of the common people the crab was a smaller, friendlier animal, about whom they liked to tell tales like this.

THERE once was a crab who had nothing better to do than watch the fish that lived in a tank nearby. There were seven fish, and each, in the opinion of the crab, was prettier than the last.

One morning the crab awoke to find that one of the fish was gone. And the one that was gone was the fat-

test and prettiest of the lot. The six that remained were huddled together at one end of the tank, and when the crab questioned them as to the whereabouts of their brother, they just turned up their eyes and cried, "Alas!"

Now it happened that a very haughty crane was standing on one leg by the river. He undertook at once to answer the crab's question. "You will learn nothing at all from those foolish fish," said the crane. "They are so frightened they have lost the best part of their wits. There were three fishermen here just now, each fiercer than the last, and they had their eyes on the fattest, the youngest, the tenderest fish. So I, being a kindly bird, carried the silly young thing to safety. That I did."

And the crane stretched his long neck and drew it in again and stood there very haughty on one leg, for all the world as though he had stood there forever.

Ah! thought the crab, if only I were as brave and noble as the crane! And he dug himself into the sand, ashamed that he had not rescued the fish himself.

The next morning the crab dug himself out of the sand and went to look at the fish. He counted them, and found that two were now missing. The five that were left were swimming about at the far end of the tank, casting up their eyes and saying, "Alas!"

The crab hurried down to the river, and there was the crane, still standing on one leg as though he had never moved.

"Lord Crane!" shouted the crab, "Lord Crane! Have the fishermen been here again?"

"They have been here, they have," answered the crane. "They had their eyes on the prettiest fish left. It was almost as fat as the first, and just as juicy and tender. So I carried it away to safety."

Now the crab was even more ashamed than before that he had not rescued the fish. He had hid in the sand all night and had never seen the fishermen. And he swore he would not sleep a wink that night, but only

watch over the fish—more carefully than ever before.

So the crab sat himself down in front of the tank and did not take his eyes off it until the moon set. Then, since there was no more light to see by, he began to feel sleepier and sleepier, and before he knew it, he was asleep.

When the sun rose, the crab awoke and jumped up, very much ashamed. He counted the fish quickly, and found to his relief that none had been taken during the night. They were swimming around happily in the tank.

Joyfully the crab hurried down to the river where the crane was standing as though he had been placed there at the beginning of the world.

"Lord Crane! Lord Crane!" shouted the crab. "The fishermen did not come last night. I sat by the tank and frightened them away."

The crane stretched his long neck and drew it in again. Then he ruffled his feathers and smoothed them with his long beak and looked at the crab.

"You are mistaken, my friend," said the crane. "The fishermen came."

"Oh," said the crab in a very small voice.

"The fishermen came, and they looked," continued the crane. "They came in the dark between the moon and the sun. They carried torches a hundred times brighter than the stars, and they waved the torches, and the torches ate up the dark until it was gone. Each fish stood out in the water like a jewel."

The crane spoke in such a loud and terrible voice that it was as though the end of the world had come. The crab turned pale and began to tremble.

"Then the fishermen found no fish to their liking?" he asked.

"They were not looking at the fish," said the crane. "They were looking at you."

Then the crab wished he had feasted his whole life on air so that he would be thin and shrunken in his shell.

"I am too fat," he sobbed. "I knew I was too fat. I am plump and tender and juicy. The fishermen will come with their baskets and carry me home to be boiled and eaten."

"Shall I carry you to safety?" asked the crane.

"If only it were possible!" sobbed the crab. "But I have promised myself I would stay and watch over the fish."

"Silly crab," said the crane, "how can you watch over the fish when you are boiling merrily away in a kettle?"

"That is true," said the crab. "That is very true."

"It is," said the crane. And with that he shot out his long neck and scooped up the crab in his beak and flew away with him.

Away and away they flew until they came to a flat rock well hidden in the reeds that grow by the river Nile. The crane tilted his wings and drifted down and laid the crab on the rock.

"Now, my friend, you are safe from the fishermen," he said.

Safe indeed! After the crab had caught his breath he looked around him. The whole rock was littered with

fish bones, and among them he recognized the bones of his friends.

"Murderer!" he shouted. "There were no fishermen! It was you who looked at the fish!"

Then a terrible battle began. The crane lunged at the crab with snapping beak. The crab clattered his claws and dashed at the crane. At last the crab managed to clamp his claws on the crane's long neck. There he clung, pinching tighter and tighter until the crane's throat was pinched so small the bird could hardly breathe. The crane's face grew redder and redder as he struggled for breath.

At last the crane begged for mercy and the crab let him go. The crane flew away until he was only a speck in the blue sky, and the crab went home to tell the fish how they had been tricked.

And that is why, to this day, the crane has a red face, and why he can swallow only small animals such as snails, and why the crab is known in Egypt as the great protector of fish.

SCRAPED-THE-BOTTOM

Here is an American version of a story that was introduced by early settlers from northern Europe. In the new country the story changed. It wandered a bit over the country. It grew longer, and acquired a happy ending in which the villain gets what he deserves.

ONE day Brother Bear went down the mountain to buy himself a keg of lard. He met Brother Fox, who wanted to know where old furry-paws was going.

The bear knew the fox was full of tricks, so he said, "I am going to buy me a bit of lard, and in case you don't know it, I don't need any help from you."

"Just the same," said the fox, "a little bit of lard seems like a little bit of nothing for a big black bear."

"It will do till the next time," the bear said, and he went along the road with the fox trotting beside him.

They had gone only a short piece when the bear stopped and said, "Brother Fox, would you look in my ear and see what is making the jingle-jangle there?"

So the fox raised himself on his tippy-toes and looked in the bear's ear. "Can't see anything but ear-wax."

"Ear-wax doesn't jingle," said the bear, and away they went.

They had gone only a little piece farther when old furry-paws stopped again. "Brother Fox," he begged, "please look in my other ear for the jingle-jangle. It's driving me half-crazy."

So the fox raised himself on his tippy-toes and looked in the bear's other ear. "Positively nothing," he said, and away they went.

Yonder, where the road straightens out, the bear stopped a third time. "That jingle-jangle is getting louder," he yelled. "It's getting so that I can't hear anything else. Don't you hear it too, Brother Fox?"

The fox cocked his head to listen and said, "Oh, *that* jingle-jangle! Must be the coins in my pocket. When I met you, I was on my way down the mountain to buy me a barrel of lard."

The bear was wondering where old sneaky-eyes got all that money for a barrel of lard.

The bear and the fox went on down the mountain, old furry-paws stepping soft and heavy, and mister sneaky-eyes dancing around to make his coins jingle. The bear kept thinking about that barrel of lard, and the longer he thought, the more he wondered if this pointy-nosed little bag-of-bones running beside him was as tricky as folks said.

And by the time they came in sight of town, he loved the fox like a brother.

"Look," said the bear, stopping dead in his tracks, "I just thought of something. If we happened to put our money together, it would stretch twice as far, and we could buy us a whopping lot of lard."

"Yes!" said the fox, and they went into the first store they came to.

But when the fox laid his money on the counter, it was nothing but copper pennies. The bear was furious. If his daddy hadn't told him long ago that a bear never breaks his bargain, he would never have put down his own money on the counter. As it was, he had no choice. He gave the store-man his coins, and the store-man counted all the money, and it came to just enough to buy a small pail of lard.

All the way back home the bear planned how he could trick mister sneaky-eyes in return. At last he said, "I'll tell you how it is. It's just too hot for lard. Why don't we save it for Christmas, when it will be good and hardened up?"

What he hoped was that the fox would get so tired of waiting he'd take himself off somewhere else.

The fox said he didn't mind waiting for his dinner, so he and the bear hid the lard in a cave. Then both of them lay down there to sleep.

When they had slept a little while, the fox awoke: "Yes," he said, then he went to the pail and dipped his nose into the lard and gobbled up a good lump of it.

When old furry-paws woke up he said to the fox, "Where have you been?" thinking his friend looked very fat in the stomach.

"Why, would you believe it, I was invited to a christening party," said the fox.

"Christening party!" said the bear. "What is the child's name?"

"Just-begun," said the fox, and threw himself down to finish his nap.

The bear yawned and turned over and was snoring again in a moment. But the fox never closed his eyes. As soon as he heard the bear's snores he said, "Yes!" and jumped up and again ran to the pail. This time he dipped his nose, and his paws, too, into the lard, and scooped out a big gob of it.

Pretty soon the bear woke up and again demanded, "Where have you been this time? You look fatter than ever."

The fox grinned and said, "You'd never believe there could be so many christenings in one night. But I was invited to another one over the hill, and they fed me gooseberry pie until I was ready to burst."

"And what was *this* child's name?" asked the bear.

"Oh, it has as strange a name as the first," said the fox. "They called it Half-empty." And with that he threw himself down and pretended to go to sleep.

As soon as the bear began to snore again, the fox ran to the lard pail and scraped it clean. This time the bear woke up suddenly and stood wagging his head angrily. "Now, where have you been? Don't talk to me about another christening, because I won't believe it."

"But that is exactly where I've been," said the fox. "Down in the valley this time, and would you believe it, there was johnny-cake and buckets of molasses to go with it, and the sweetest pickles ever."

"And the child's name was —" the bear began, but the fox yelled, "Scraped-the-bottom!" before the bear could finish.

"Now listen to me!" said the bear. "I just don't believe you now at all. I don't think you've been to *one* single christening, let alone *three*. I think you've been sneaking over to sample the lard."

At that the fox pulled a long face and said, "How can you think that? If you weren't close as a brother to me, I'd bite you in two."

"Then show me the pail of lard," demanded the bear.

"Gladly," said the fox, and skipped over to where it was hidden. He suddenly began kicking the empty pail around, yelling at the top of his voice, "Thief! Thief! You stole the lard while I was at the christening parties!"

"Not I," said the bear. "There weren't any christening parties, and you weren't at them."

Just then Brother Owl spoke from the corner of the cave where he had been sitting all night long watching the fox. "I know how to settle this quarrel," he said.

"Both of you go out to the hillside and go to sleep. When the sun comes up, it will melt the lard on the thief's whiskers, and we'll know him by his greasy muzzle."

So the bear and the fox went out to the hillside to sleep.

As soon as he was sure the bear was asleep, the fox polished his whiskers until there wasn't one bit of lard left on them. Then he closed his eyes, too.

Meanwhile, the owl flew into the cave, found a tiny piece of lard on the floor, and carried it to the hillside. He smeared it very carefully on the fox's whiskers. Then he settled himself in a tree and never took his eyes off mister sly-boots the rest of the night.

The next morning the fox awoke with his muzzle all greasy. The owl cried, "Thief!" The bear cried, "Thief!" Then both of them chased the fox over the mountains so far he never found his way back.

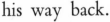

THE UGLY DUCKLING

by HANS CHRISTIAN ANDERSEN

*Perhaps the best of all possible stories is that in which ugliness
is changed into beauty. Here it is as one of the world's best-
loved storytellers told it.*

SUMMERTIME! How lovely it was out in the country,
with the wheat standing yellow, the oats green, and the
hay all stacked down in the grassy meadows! And there
went the stork on his long red legs, chattering away in
Egyptian, for he had learned that language from his
mother. The fields and meadows had large woods all
around, and in the middle of the woods there were deep
lakes.

Yes, it certainly was lovely out in the country. Bathed
in sunshine stood an old manor-house with a deep moat

round it, and growing out of the wall down by the water were huge dock leaves. The biggest of them were so tall that little children could stand upright underneath. The place was as tangled and twisty as the densest forest, and here it was that a duck was sitting on her nest. It was time for her to hatch out her little ducklings, but it was such a long job that she was beginning to lose patience. She hardly ever had a visitor. The other ducks thought more of swimming about in the moat than of coming and sitting under a dock leaf just for the sake of a quack with her.

At last the eggs cracked open one after the other—"peep! peep!"—and all the yolks had come to life and were sticking out their heads.

"Quack, quack!" said the mother duck, and then the little ones scuttled out as quickly as they could, prying all round under the green leaves; and she let them do this as much as they liked, because green is so good for the eyes.

"Oh, how big the world is!" said the ducklings. They certainly had much more room now than when they were lying in the egg.

"Do you suppose this is the whole world?" said their mother. "Why, it goes a long way past the other side of the garden, right into the parson's field. But I've never been as far as that. Well, you're all out now, I hope." And she got up from her nest. "No, not all. The largest egg is still here. How long will it be? I can't bother about it much more." And she went on sitting again.

"Well, how's it going?" asked an old duck who came to pay a call.

"There's just this one egg that's taking such a long time," said the sitting duck. "It simply won't break. But just look at the others—the loveliest duck-lings I've ever seen. They all take after their father—the wretch! Why doesn't he come and see me?"

"Let's have a look at the egg that won't crack," said the old duck. "I'll bet it's a turkey's egg. That's how I was bamboozled once. The little ones gave me no end of trouble, for they were afraid of the water—fancy that! I just couldn't get them to go in. I quacked and clacked, but it was no good. Let's have a look at the egg... Aye, that's a turkey's egg, depend upon it! Let it be, and teach the others to swim."

"I think I'll sit just a little while yet," said the duck. "I've been sitting so long that it won't hurt to sit a little longer."

"Please yourself!" said the old duck, and away she waddled.

At last the big egg cracked. There was a "peep! peep!" from the young one as he tumbled out, looking so large and ugly. The duck glanced at him and said, "My! what a huge great duckling that is! None of the others look a bit like that. Still, it's never a turkey-chick, I'll be bound... Well, we shall soon find out. He shall go into the water if I have to kick him in myself."

The next day the weather was gloriously fine, with sun shining on all the green dock leaves. The mother duck with her whole family came down to the moat. Splash! into the water she jumped. "Quack, quack!" she said, and one after another the ducklings plopped in after her. The water closed over their heads, but they were up again in a moment and floated along so beautifully. Their legs worked of their own accord, and now

the whole lot were in the water—even the ugly gray duckling joined in the swimming.

"It's no turkey, that's certain," said the duck. "Look how beautifully he uses his legs and how straight he holds himself. He's my own little one all right, and he's quite handsome, when you really come to look at him. Quack, quack! Now, come along with me and let me show you the world and introduce you all to the barn-yard, but mind and keep close to me, so that nobody steps on you. And keep a sharp lookout for the cat."

Then they made their way into the duck yard. There was a fearful noise going on, for two families were fighting for an eel's head, finally the cat got it.

"You see! That's the way of the world," said the mother duck and licked her beak, for she too had fancied the eel's head. "Now then, where are your legs?" she said. "Look slippy and make a nice bow to the old duck over there. She's the most genteel of all these. She has Spanish blood, that's why she's so plump. And do you see that crimson rag she wears on one leg? It's extremely fine. It's the highest distinction any duck can win. It's as good as saying that there is no thought of getting rid of her. Man and beast are to take notice! Look alive, and don't turn your toes in! A well-bred duckling turns it's toes out, like father and mother . . . that's it. Now make a bow and say 'quack!'"

They all obeyed. But the other ducks round about looked at them and said out loud, "There! Now we've got to have that rabble as well—as if there weren't enough of us already! Ugh! What a sight that duckling

is! We can't possibly put up with him." And one duck immediately flew at him and bit him in the neck.

"Let him alone," said the mother. "He's doing no one any harm."

"Yes, but he's so gawky and peculiar," said the one that had pecked him, "so he'll have to be squashed."

"What pretty children you have, my dear!" said the old duck with the rag on her leg. "All of them but one, who doesn't seem right. I only wish you could make him all over again."

"No question of that, my lady," said the ducklings' mother. "He's not pretty, but he's so good-tempered and he can swim just as well as the others—I daresay even a bit better. I fancy his looks will improve as he grows up, or maybe in time he'll grow down a little. He lay too long in the egg—that's why he isn't quite the right shape." And then she plucked his neck for him and smoothed out his feathers. "Anyhow, he's a drake, and so it doesn't matter so much," she added. "I feel sure he'll turn out pretty strong and be able to manage all right."

"The other ducklings are charming," said the old duck. "Make yourselves at home, my dears, and if you should find such a thing as an eel's head, you may bring it to me."

And so they made themselves at home.

But the poor duckling who was the last out of the egg and looked so ugly got pecked and jostled and teased by ducks and hens alike. "The great gawk!" they all clucked. And the turkey, who was born with spurs and therefore thought himself an emperor, puffed up his feathers like a ship under full sail and went straight at him, and then he gobble-gobbled till he was quite red in the face. The poor duckling didn't know where to turn. He was terribly upset over being so ugly and the laughing-stock of the whole barnyard.

That's how it was the first day, and afterwards things grew worse and worse. The poor duckling got pushed about by all of them. Even his own brothers and sisters treated him badly, and they kept saying, "If only the cat would get you, you ridiculous great guy!" And the mother herself wished he were far away. The ducks nipped him, the hens pecked him, and the maid who had to feed the poultry let fly at him with her foot.

After that, he ran away and fluttered over the hedge, and the little birds in the bushes grew frightened and flew into the air. "That's because I'm so ugly," thought the duckling, and closed his eyes—and yet managed to get away. Eventually he came out to the great marsh where the wild ducks lived, and lay there all night, utterly tired and completely dispirited.

In the morning the wild ducks flew up and looked at their new companion. "Whatever are you?" they asked, and the duckling turned in every direction and bowed as well as he could.

"What a scarecrow you are!" said the wild ducks. "But that won't matter to us, as long as you don't marry into our family." Poor thing! He wasn't dreaming of getting married. All he wanted was to be allowed to stay quietly among the rushes and drink a little marsh water. After he had been there for two whole days, two wild geese came along—or rather, two wild ganders, for they were both males. It was not long since they had been hatched. That's why they were so perky.

"Look here, my lad!" they began. "You are so ugly that we quite like you. Will you come in with us and migrate? Not far off, in another marsh, are some very nice young wild geese, none of them married, who can quack beautifully. Here's a chance for you to make a hit, ugly as you are."

"Bang! bang!" suddenly echoed above them, and both the ganders fell down dead in the rushes, and the water became red with blood. "Bang! bang!" sounded once more, and flocks of wild geese flew up from the rushes, so that immediately fresh shots rang out. A big shoot was on. The hunting party lay ready all round the marsh; some even sat up in the trees on the branches that stretched right out over the rushes. Clouds of blue smoke drifted in among the dark trees and hung far over the water. Splashing through the

185

mud came the gun-dogs, bending back reeds and rushes
this way and that. It was terrifying for the poor duckling,
who was just turning his head round to bury it under
his wing when he suddenly found close beside him a
fearsome great dog with lolling tongue and grim,
glittering eyes. It lowered its muzzle right down to the
duckling, bared its sharp teeth and—splash! It went off
again without touching him.

The duckling gave a sigh of relief. "Thank goodness, I'm so ugly that even the dog doesn't fancy the taste of me." And he lay there quite still, while the shot pattered on the reeds and crack after crack was heard from the guns.

It was late in the day before everything was quiet again, but the poor duckling didn't dare to get up yet. He waited several hours longer before he took a look round and then made off from the marsh as fast as he could go. Over field and meadow he scuttled, but there was such a wind that he found it difficult to get along.

Toward evening he came up to a poor little farm cottage. It was so broken down that it hardly knew which way to fall, and so it remained standing. The wind whizzed so fiercely round the duckling that he had to sit on his tail so as not to be blown over. The wind grew worse and worse. Then he noticed that the door had come off one of its hinges and hung so much on the slant that he could slip into the house through the crack. And that's just what he did.

There was an old woman living there with her cat and her hen. The cat, whom she called Sonny, could arch its back and purr. It could even give out sparks, if you stroked its fur the wrong way. The hen had such short little legs that it was called Chickabiddy Shortlegs. It was a very good layer, and the woman loved it like her own child.

Next morning they at once noticed the strange duck-ling, and the cat started to purr and the hen to cluck. "Why, what's up?" said the woman, looking round. But her sight wasn't very good, and she took the duckling for a fat duck that had lost its way. "My! What a find!" she said. "I shall be able to have duck's eggs—as long as it isn't a drake! Let's give it a trial."

And so the duckling was taken on trial for three weeks. But there was no sign of an egg. Now, the cat was master in the house and the hen was mistress, and they always used to say "We and the world," because they fancied that they made up half the world—what's more, much the superior half of it. The duckling thought there might be two opinions about that, but the hen wouldn't hear of it.

"Can you lay eggs?" she asked.

"No."

"Well, then, hold your tongue, will you!"

And the cat asked: "Can you arch your back or purr or give out sparks?"

"No."

"Well, then, your opinion's not wanted, when sensible people are talking."

And the duckling sat in the corner, quite out of spirits. Then suddenly he remembered the fresh air and the sunshine, and he got such a curious longing to swim in the water that—he couldn't help it—he had to tell the hen.

"What's the matter with you?" she asked. "You haven't anything to do—that's why you get these fancies. They'd go, if only you'd lay eggs or else purr."

"But it's so lovely to swim in the water," said the duckling; "so lovely to duck your head in it and dive down to the bottom."

"Most enjoyable, I'm sure," said the hen. "You must have gone crazy. Ask the cat about it—I've never met anyone as clever as he is—ask him if he's fond of swimming or diving! I say nothing of myself. Ask our old mistress, the wisest woman in the world! Do you suppose that she's keen on swimming and diving?"

"You don't understand me," said the duckling.

"Well, if we don't understand you, I should like to know who would. Surely you'll never try and make out you are wiser than the cat and the mistress—not to mention myself. Don't be silly, child! Give thanks to your Maker for all the kindness you have met with. Haven't you come to a nice warm room, where you have company that can teach you something? But you're just a stupid duck, and there's no fun in having you here. You may take my word for it—if I say unpleasant things to you, it's all for your good. That's just how you can tell which are your real friends. Only see that you lay eggs and learn how to purr or give out sparks!"

"I think I'll go out into the wide world," said the duckling.

"Yes, do," said the hen.

And so the duckling went off. He swam in the water; he dived down; but nobody would have anything to do with him because of his ugliness.

Autumn now set in. The leaves in the wood turned yellow and brown, the wind seized them and whirled them about, while the sky above had a frosty look. The clouds hung heavy with hail and snow, and the raven who perched on the fence kept squawking, "Ow! Ow!"—he felt so cold. The very thought of it gave you the shivers. Yes, the poor duckling was certainly having a bad time.

One evening, when there was a lovely sunset, a whole flock of large handsome birds appeared out of the bushes. The duckling had never seen such beautiful birds, all glittering white with long graceful necks. They were swans. They gave the most extraordinary cry, spread out their magnificent long wings and flew from this cold country away to warmer lands and open lakes. They mounted high, high up into the air, and the ugly little duckling felt so strange as he watched them. He turned round and round in the water like a wheel and craned his neck in their direction, letting out a cry so shrill and strange that it quite scared even himself. Ah! he could never forget those beautiful, fortunate birds. Directly they were lost to sight he dived right down to the bottom and, when he came up again, he was almost beside himself. He had no idea what the birds were called, nor where they were flying to, and yet they were dearer to him than any he had ever known. He didn't envy them in the least—how could he ever dream of such loveliness for himself? He would be quite satisfied if only the ducks would just put up with him, poor gawky-looking creature!

What a cold winter it was! The duckling had to keep swimming about in the water to prevent it freezing right up. But every night the pool he was swimming in grew smaller and smaller. Then the ice froze so

hard that you could hear it cracking. The duckling had to keep his feet moving all the time to prevent the water from closing up. At last he grew faint with exhaustion and lay quite still and finally froze fast in the ice.

Early next morning he was seen by a peasant who went out and broke the ice with his wooden clog and carried the duckling home to his wife. And there they revived him.

The children wanted to play with him, but the duckling was afraid they meant mischief and fluttered in panic right up into the milk bowl, so that the milk slopped over into the room. The woman screamed out and clapped her hands in the air, and then he flew into the butter tub, and from there down into the flour bin, and out of it again. Dear, dear, he did look

an object! The woman screamed at him and hit at him with the tongs, and the children tumbled over each other trying to catch him—how they laughed and shouted! . . . It was a good thing the door was open. The duckling darted out into the bushes and sank down, dazed, in the new-fallen snow.

But it would be far too dismal to describe all the want and misery the duckling had to go through during that hard winter.

He was sheltering among the reeds on the marsh, when the sun began to get warm again and the larks to sing: beautiful spring had arrived.

Then all at once he tried his wings. The whirr of them was louder than before, and they carried him swiftly away. Almost before he realized it, he found himself in a big garden with apple trees in blossom and sweet-smelling lilac that dangled from long green boughs right over the winding stream. Oh, it was so lovely here in all the freshness of spring! And straight ahead, out of the thicket, came three beautiful white swans, ruffling their feathers and floating so lightly on the water. The duckling recognized the splendid creatures and was overcome with a strange feeling of melancholy.

"I will fly across to them, those royal birds! They will peck me to death for daring, ugly as I am, to go near them. Never mind! Better to be killed by them than be nipped by the ducks, pecked by the hens, kicked by the girl who minds the poultry, and made to suffer hardship in winter."

And he flew out to the water and swam toward the

beautiful swans. As they caught sight of him, they darted
with ruffled feathers to meet him.

"Yes, kill me, do kill me!" cried the poor creature and
bowed his head to the water awaiting death. But what
did he see there in the clear stream? It was a reflection

of himself that he saw in front of him, but no longer
a clumsy grayish bird, ugly and unattractive—no, he
was himself a swan!

It doesn't matter about being born in a duck yard,
as long as you are hatched from a swan's egg.

He felt positively glad at having gone through so much hardship and want. It helped him to appreciate all the happiness and beauty that were there to welcome him. . . . And the three great swans swam round and round and stroked him with their beaks.

Some little children came into the garden and threw bread and grain into the water, and the smallest one called out, "There's a new swan!" And the other children joined in with shouts of delight: "Yes, there's a new swan!" And they clapped their hands and danced about and ran to fetch father and mother. Bits of bread and cake were thrown into the water, and everyone said, "The new one is the prettiest—so young and handsome!" And the old swans bowed before him.

This made him feel quite shy, and he tucked his head away under his wing—he himself hardly knew why. He was too, too happy, but not a bit proud, for a good heart is never proud. He thought of how he had been despised and persecuted, and now he heard everybody saying that he was the loveliest of all lovely birds. And the lilacs bowed their branches to him right down to the water, and the sunshine felt so warm and kindly. Then he ruffled his feathers, raised his slender neck and rejoiced from his heart: "I never dreamed of so much happiness, when I was the ugly duckling."

TWO FROGS FROM JAPAN

*If you look carefully at the next frog you meet, you will under-
stand why this story ends as it does.*

TWO frogs lived on the island of Hondo in Japan. One
lived in a ditch outside the city of Osaka, while the other
lived in a crystal clear stream near Kioto.

Neither frog knew anything about the other, for
between them lay a high mountain. But on the very same
day, at the very same moment, each frog decided he
would climb over the mountain to visit the city that lay
on the other side. The frog from Osaka wanted to see
the city of Kioto where the Mikado had his palace. The
frog from Kioto wanted to see Osaka, where there
were no palaces at all.

The next morning, early, the two frogs set out, lep-
lep-lep. The one went up this side of the mountain, the
other went up that. The way was long and hard, but
at last they came over the top of the mountain at the
very same moment in the very same place. Each frog
sat down in the tall grass and stared at the other for a
long time.

At last the frog from Osaka asked, "Where are you

going, O most distinguished of explorers?"

The frog from Kioto harrumphed in his throat a few times before he answered, "I am going to Osaka, O most gracious of explorers."

"Indeed!" exclaimed the frog from Osaka. "Then let me tell you that it is not worth your trouble. I come from there myself, and it is a poor place, full of ditch water. As for me, I am going to visit Kioto."

"Kioto indeed!" harrumphed the frog from that place. "It is true there is no ditch water in Kioto, but have you ever lived in a stream that sparkles all day long? It is very hard on the eyes."

And the two frogs sat and stared at each other, saying nothing, for another long time.

Then the frog from Osaka sighed and said, "Having climbed one side of the mountain, I do not want to climb down the other side if there is nothing worth seeing below. If only we were taller animals we could look down from this great height and see if the city we are bound for is worth our journey. But alas, I cannot see over this tall grass, and neither can you."

The frog from Kioto puffed out his throat in a most impressive way and said, "Well, we can settle that, my friend. It is true we are both very small, but we frogs from Kioto are famous for our intelligence. Let me think awhile."

So the frog from Kioto closed his eyes and thought and thought, and at last he said, "I have settled it. If you will help me to stand on my hind legs, I will help you to stand on yours. Then we shall both be taller than the

grass and each can look down on the city he wants to visit."

So the frog from Osaka faced toward the city of Kioto, and the frog from Kioto faced toward Osaka. Then each helped the other to stand on his hind legs and held him fast with his short forelegs. In this manner the two frogs stood facing each other for a long time, each studying a different city and lost in his own thoughts.

But the foolish frogs had forgotten one thing. Both had forgotten that their huge eyes lay almost on the top of their heads. Each had faced the city of his dreams while he was sitting down. But now that he was standing up, his eyes were facing backwards. Each frog was now looking at the city he had just come from.

"Ah!" exclaimed the frog from Osaka. "What do I
see here? Kioto looks like the twin sister of my old Osaka.
I may just as well save myself the journey."

"Ah!" exclaimed the frog from Kioto. "What do I
see? Osaka looks just like Kioto. Now I may as well save
myself the trouble of going there."

And with that each frog let go of the other and they
both fell *bump* into the tall grass. Then, being Japanese,
they bowed to each other and went their separate ways
homeward.

Until the last day of their lives the two frogs of Japan
believed that the cities of Kioto and Osaka were as alike
as two eggs. Neither frog ever learned that he had been
mistaken.

CLEVER BROTHER HARE

There are many, many folk tales about animals, and people, too, who escape from danger by using their wits. Here is one from Africa.

MANY years ago, in a country where there were as yet no people, all the animals lived happily together. They never argued, and they never ate each other up.

Then one day Brother Lion appeared in the forest. He was very proud and very strong, and soon he began to quarrel with the other animals just to show them he was better than they. Before long he killed some of them.

The animals were very angry with Brother Lion but, because he was so strong, they dared not complain. They did not know what to do. And then one day Brother Lion proclaimed himself king of the whole country and made Brother Jackal his prime minister.

206

Now Brother Jackal was no more loved by the other animals than was Brother Lion. He was a flatterer, and a great coward as well. He always told Brother Lion just what he wanted to hear and what pleased him most. In return, Brother Lion gave Brother Jackal everything he did not want himself. Brother Jackal had a fine time.

One day Brother Lion decided that each of the animals in turn must bring him a hot meal every evening. He sent Brother Jackal into the forest to announce his decision. Brother Jackal took a great trumpet, and walked up and down the land blowing it, announcing Brother Lion's command.

The animals were all so angry that they did not sleep a wink that night, but not one of them dared stand up to Brother Lion and refuse to bring him his dinner. Brother Jackal walked up and down the land, blowing his trumpet and calling out his message, and nobody even argued with him.

So every evening after that Brother Lion was given a fine roast joint for his dinner. He ate it in his cave, thinking all the while what a high and mighty fellow he was. Brother Jackal sat beside him, praising him to the skies, sure of a share of the food when Brother Lion had eaten his fill.

At last all the animals had served Brother Lion a meal except Brother Hare. He was sitting peacefully in his house with his wife and children when Brother Jackal came along the street playing loudly on his trumpet.

"Are you there, Brother Hare?" he cried.

"Yes, I am here, " Brother Hare answered.

"Have you obeyed Brother Lion's command?"

"What command, Brother Jackal?" asked Brother Hare, just as though he knew nothing about it.

"Why, that it's your turn to bring him a meal this evening," answered Brother Jackal, a grin spreading all over his face. "And it must be well prepared, too, or Brother Lion will eat you up together with Mrs. Hare and all your children. So hurry up and do your duty."

"Good, Brother Jackal," replied Brother Hare. "Go and tell your master that I will be there promptly with his dinner."

And then he picked up the bucket which was full of water and emptied it, so that the room was swimming in water and the jackal's feet got wet.

Brother Jackal was very cross about his wet stockings and went off saying to himself with a sneer, "The little hare will never be able to provide the big lion with enough to eat. He will be eaten up himself. True, he won't make more than a little snack, but what a tender, tasty snack he will be!"

Meanwhile, the hare was peacefully scrubbing his house and singing to himself in a most cheerful way.

Presently the door opened and in came Mrs. Hare and her children. They were all holding their handkerchiefs to their eyes and weeping bitterly.

"What's this? What's the matter?" demanded Brother Hare in astonishment.

"Oh dear! Oh dear!" wailed Mrs. Hare. "We heard what Brother Jackal said. Now Brother Lion will eat us all up, for how can we possibly get a big enough meal for him?"

"Don't worry," said the hare, comforting her. "And you children be quiet now. Have no fear, the lion won't eat either you or me."

Thereupon Brother Hare asked for a bowl of warm water, washed himself very carefully, put on his best suit, chose his prettiest tie, twirled the ends of his whiskers, and left the house with his walking stick under his arm.

When the other animals saw the hare all dressed up they ran to their doors and called out, "Brother Hare! Where are you going in your best clothes?"

"Good evening, my friends," answered the hare. "I am on my way to see the lion to bring him to his senses. Brother Jackal has just been on his rounds, and if what he says is true, Brother Lion must have lost his mind."

"Oh, don't go near that terrible fellow!" begged all the animals. "You will surely be eaten up!"

But Brother Hare twisted his whiskers, swung his little stick, and went calmly along the path that led to the lion's cave. As soon as he was out of sight of the other animals he ruffled his hair, loosened his tie, and rolled around in the dust until he looked like someone who has been waylaid and beaten. Then he went on to the lion's cave.

Brother Lion was sitting writing inside. He was in a terrible rage because his dinner was late. When he saw Brother Hare coming through his front door he roared, "What is the meaning of this? How dare you keep me waiting for my supper? Now I shall eat you up!"

And he opened his mouth so wide that Brother Jackal crept quietly out and put as much distance as possible between himself and his master.

Brother Hare, however, did not move so much as an inch. He looked at Brother Lion with the saddest face

and said in a doleful voice, "Oh, Brother Lion, please forgive me, it is not my fault. I had such a splendid meal for you. Mrs. Hare prepared it herself with the greatest care, and she is an excellent cook. But as I was carrying this delicious food to you, a great big lion came out of the bushes and took it all away. I told him it was for you and that you were the king of all the animals, but he only roared the louder and said he was the only king here. He said I was to tell you this, and then he swallowed all the food."

Brother Lion let out a terrible roar and beat the ground with his tail. "Where is this scoundrel that calls himself king of the animals?" he roared. "Show me his hiding place! Take me to it. I will tear him to pieces!"

"I told him that already," said Brother Hare, "but he only laughed at me."

And so the two set out to find the hiding place of the scoundrel lion. The hare ran ahead, and Brother Lion stamped along after him. Soon they came to a deep hole full of water. Here the hare stopped.

"Your enemy lives in this hole, Brother Lion," he said. "I dare not go nearer, because I am so small. But if you bend down and look into the hole, you will see him. Take care that the dreadful beast does not leap out and eat you up!"

The lion stepped to the edge of the hole. He looked down and saw his own reflection in the water.

"So there you are!" he screamed, baring his teeth.

The lion in the water did the same thing!

"I will tear you into a thousand pieces!" roared Brother Lion, flying into a still greater rage.

The lion in the water did the same thing!

In his anger, Brother Lion bent low to seize his enemy, and his enemy rose up to seize him. Brother Lion sprang at his enemy, and *plop*! he fell into the water. Only then did he realize that Brother Hare had tricked him.

Brother Lion tried hard to save himself, but the sides of the hole were so steep that he could not climb out.

Brother Hare brushed his dusty clothes, twirled his whiskers, and started for home, swinging his stick and singing, "Tolderollree! The villain will fall into his own snare!"

HENNY-PENNY

by JOSEPH JACOBS

Thousands and thousands of children have enjoyed this funny English story of the hen who thought the sky was falling. But how many know that it is one of the oldest folk tales we have, and that it came originally from India? In the Indian story the hen is a rabbit.

ONE day Henny-Penny was picking up corn in the barnyard when—whack!—something hit her on the head. "Goodness gracious me!" said Henny-Penny, "the sky's a-going to fall. I must go and tell the King."

So she went along, and she went along, and she went along till she met Cocky-Locky. "Where are you going, Henny-Penny?" says Cocky-Locky.

"Oh! I'm going to tell the King the sky's a-falling," says Henny-Penny.

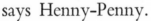

"May I come with you?" says Cocky-Locky.

"Certainly," says Henny-Penny. So Henny-Penny and Cocky-Locky went to tell the King the sky was a-falling.

They went along, and they went along, and they went along till they met Ducky-Lucky. "Where are you going, Henny-Penny and Cocky-Locky?" says Ducky-Lucky.

"Oh, we're going to tell the King the sky's a-falling," said Henny-Penny and Cocky-Locky.

"May I come with you?" says Ducky-Lucky.

"Certainly," said Henny-Penny and Cocky-Locky. So Henny-Penny, Cocky-Locky, and Ducky-Lucky went to tell the King the sky was a-falling.

So they went along, and they went along, and they went along until they met Goosey-Poosey. "Where are you going to, Henny-Penny, Cocky-Locky, and Ducky-Lucky?" said Goosey-Poosey.

"Oh, we're going to tell the King the sky's a-falling," said Henny-Penny, Cocky-Locky, and Ducky-Lucky.

"May I come with you?" said Goosey-Poosey.

"Certainly," said Henny-Penny, Cocky-Locky, and Ducky-Lucky. So Henny-Penny, Cocky-Locky, Ducky-Lucky, and Goosey-Poosey went to tell the King the sky was a-falling.

So they went along, and they went along, and they went along till they met Turkey-Lurkey. "Where are you going, Henny-Penny, Cocky-Locky, Ducky-Lucky, and Goosey-Poosey?" said Turkey-Lurkey.

"Oh, we're going to tell the King the sky's a-falling," said Henny-Penny, Cocky-Locky, Ducky-Lucky, and Goosey-Poosey.

"May I come with you, Henny-Penny, Cocky-Locky, Ducky-Lucky, and Goosey-Poosey?" said Turkey-Lurkey.

"Oh, certainly, Turkey-Lurkey," said Henny-Penny, Cocky-Locky, Ducky-Lucky, and Goosey-Poosey. So Henny-Penny, Cocky-Locky, Ducky-Lucky, Goosey-Poosey, and Turkey-Lurkey all went to tell the King the sky was a-falling.

So they went along, and they went along, and they went along until they met Foxy-Woxy, and Foxy-Woxy said to Henny-Penny, Cocky-Locky, Ducky-Lucky, Goosey-Poosey, and Turkey-Lurkey, "Where are you going, Henny-Penny, Cocky-Locky, Ducky-Lucky, Goosey-Poosey, and Turkey-Lurkey?"

And Henny-Penny, Cocky-Locky, Ducky-Lucky, Goosey-Poosey, and Turkey-Lurkey said to Foxy-Woxy, "We're going to tell the King the sky's a-falling."

"Oh, but this is not the way to the King, Henny-Penny, Cocky-Locky, Ducky-Lucky, Goosey-Poosey, and Turkey-Lurkey," says Foxy-Woxy. "I know the proper way. Shall I show it to you?"

"Oh, certainly, Foxy-Woxy," said Henny-Penny, Cocky-Locky, Ducky-Lucky, Goosey-Poosey, and Turkey-Lurkey. So Henny-Penny, Cocky-Locky, Ducky Lucky, Goosey-Poosey, Turkey-Lurkey, and Foxy-Woxy all went to tell the King the sky was a-falling.

They went along and they went along, till they came to a dark, narrow hole. Now this was the door of Foxy-Woxy's cave. But Foxy-Woxy said to Henny-Penny, Cocky-Locky, Ducky-Lucky, Goosey-Poosey, and Turkey-Lurkey, "This is the short way to the King's palace. You'll soon get there. Follow me. I will go first, and you come after, Henny-Penny, Cocky-Locky, Ducky-Lucky, Goosey-Poosey, and Turkey-Lurkey."

"Why, of course, certainly, without doubt, why not?" said Henny-Penny, Cocky-Locky, Ducky-Lucky, Goosey-Poosey, and Turkey-Lurkey.

So Foxy-Woxy went into his cave, and he didn't go very far. He turned around to wait for Henny-Penny, Cocky-Locky, Ducky-Lucky, Goosey-Poosey, and Turkey-Lurkey.

First Turkey-Lurkey went through the dark hole into the cave. He hadn't got far when "*Hrumph*," Foxy-Woxy snapped off Turkey-Lurkey's head and threw his body over his left shoulder.

Then Goosey-Poosey went in, and "*Hrumph*," off went her head, and Goosey-Poosey was thrown beside Turkey-Lurkey.

Then Ducky-Lucky waddled in, and "*Hrumph*," snapped Foxy-Woxy, and Ducky-Lucky's head was off and Ducky-Lucky was thrown alongside Turkey-Lurkey and Goosey-Poosey.

Then Cocky-Locky strutted down into the cave, and he hadn't gone far when "*Snap, hrumph!*" went Foxy-Woxy, and Cocky-Locky was thrown alongside Turkey-Lurkey, Goosey-Poosey, and Ducky-Lucky.

But Foxy-Woxy had made two bites at Cocky-Locky, and Cocky-Locky had time between bites to call out to Henny-Penny to go home. So Henny-Penny turned tail and ran all the way home, and she never told the King the sky was a-falling.

THE THREE BILLY-GOATS GRUFF

*It is easy to guess where this story comes from. There is a troll
in it, and who ever heard of a troll except in the Scandinavian
countries?*

ONCE upon a time there were three billy-goats who
were to go up to the hillside to make themselves fat,
and the name of all three was "Gruff."

On the way up was a bridge over a stream they had
to cross. Under the bridge lived a great ugly Troll,
with eyes as big as saucers, and a nose as long as a poker.

So first of all came the youngest billy-goat Gruff to
cross the bridge.

"Trip, trap! trip, trap!" went the bridge.

"Who's tripping over my bridge?" roared the Troll.

"Oh! It is only I, the tiniest billy-goat Gruff. And
I'm going up to the hillside to make myself fat," said
the billy-goat, with such a small voice.

"Now, I'm going to gobble you up," said the Troll.

"Oh, no! Pray don't take me. I'm too little, that
I am," said the billy-goat. "Wait a bit till the second
billy-goat Gruff comes, he's much bigger."

"Well! Be off with you," said the Troll.

A little while after came the second billy-goat Gruff
to cross the bridge.

"Trip, trap! Trip, trap! Trip, trap!" went the bridge.

"Who's tripping over my bridge?" roared the Troll.

"Oh! It's the second billy-goat Gruff, and I'm going
up to the hillside to make myself fat," said the billy-
goat, who hadn't such a small voice.

"Now, I'm going to gobble you up," said the Troll.

"Oh, no! Don't take me. Wait a little till the big billy-goat Gruff comes, he's much bigger."

"Very well! Be off with you," said the Troll.

But just then up came the big billy-goat Gruff.

"Trip, trap! Trip, trap! Trip, trap!" went the bridge, for the billy-goat was so heavy that the bridge creaked and groaned under him.

"Who's tramping over my bridge?" roared the Troll.

"It's I! The big billy-goat Gruff," said the billy-goat, who had an ugly hoarse voice of his own.

"Now, I'm going to gobble you up," roared the Troll.

"Well, come along! I've got two spears,
And I'll poke your eyeballs out at your ears;
I've got besides two curling-stones,
And I'll crush you to bits, body and bones."

That was what the big billy-goat said. And so he flew at the Troll and poked his eyes out with his horns, and crushed him to bits, body and bones, and tossed him away out into the deepest part of the stream.

Afterwards the big billy-goat went up the hillside. There the three billy-goats got so fat they could hardly walk home again. And if the fat has not fallen off them, why they're still fat. And so—

> "Snip, snap, snout,
> This tale's told out."

WHY THE BEAR
IS STUMPY-TAILED

Can you think of a better reason why the bear has a short tail?

ONE day the bear met the fox, who came slinking along with a string of fish he had stolen.

"Where did you get those from?" asked the bear.

"Oh, my Lord Bruin, I've been out fishing and caught them," said the fox.

So the bear thought he would like to learn to fish too, and he asked the fox to tell him how to go about it.

"It's easy," said the fox. "You just go out on the ice and cut a hole and stick your tail in the hole. Then you must go on holding your tail there as long as you can. You must not mind if your tail hurts a little, because that's when the fish bite. The longer you sit with your tail in the hole, the more fish you'll get. Then all at once out with your tail with a cross pull sideways, and with a strong pull, too."

The bear did what the fox had told him to do. He held his tail down in the hole a long, long time until it was frozen fast. Then he pulled it out with a cross pull, and it snapped off. And that's why the bear has such a short tail.

LITTLE HALF-CHICK

This story of a foolish little chicken comes from Spain.

THE white hen was proud of her chicks. One by one the twelve beautiful little balls of fluff had pecked their way out of their shells. Already they were running around the barnyard on their rosy little legs. And now still another chick was knocking on its shell.

"This last one is bound to be the most beautiful of all," boasted the white hen.

But when the chick at last pecked his way into the world, he was not beautiful at all. He had only one leg and one wing and one eye.

"This is strange," said the white hen. "There has never been a half-chick in my family. But at least he is distinguished. There is not another like him in the world."

And she gave him the high-sounding name of Medio Pollito, which is Spanish for little half-chick.

As the days went by the white hen grew fonder of Medio Pollito than she was of any of her other chicks. She gave him the longest worms and the fattest grains of

corn. When he scrapped with the other chicks over a
beetle or a fly, she chased them away while he gobbled
the insect up. And she was continually calling the other
barnyard animals to observe how beautifully he hopped
around on his one little leg.

Before long Medio Pollito began to believe he was as remarkable as his mother thought him. He strutted on his one leg and puffed out his chest. He was rude to his brothers and sisters and even to the dog, who was king of the barnyard. Things came to such a pass that his mother had to scold him.

"Really, Medio Pollito," she said, "everyone knows that you are the most distinguished of my chicks, but it is not polite to call attention to yourself in this way."

"Bother politeness," said Medio Pollito. "If I am distinguished, I am distinguished. The sooner the world knows it, the better."

And he began to complain about the smallness of the barnyard and the lack of distinguished company.

"After all," he said, "there is a bigger world beyond the fence. Why should a distinguished chick like me spend his life in a barnyard?"

"Ar-kuh-kuh-kuh!" clucked the white hen. "Boasting will get you nowhere. Stay with me and I shall find you the biggest worms and admire you all day long."

"That is not enough for me," said Medio Pollito. "I'm off to see the world this very day."

And with that he lifted his one little wing and flew over the fence.

Medio Pollito hopped along all day on his one leg without seeing anything he had not seen before. At last he came to a place where gypsies had camped. There, in the ashes of their fire, a single spark was trying to burn.

"Medio Pollito!" cried the spark. "Fan me, fan me, before I go out altogether."

"Go out for all of me," said Medio Pollito. "I'm off to see the world, and I have no time to stop."

And away he went, hippity-hop, on his one leg. He hopped and hopped, but still he saw nothing he had not seen before. At last he came to a stream all choked with sticks and leaves.

"Help me! Help me!" begged the stream. "Please clear away this rubbish so that I can flow back to my mother, the sea."

"Clear them away yourself," said Medio Pollito. "I have no time to stop. I'm off to see the world."

And away he went, hippity-hop, until he came to a wood where night had already fallen. It was dark and cold, and the wind was crying in the treetops.

"Medio Pollito, Medio Pollito!" cried the wind. "Please help me. Untangle me from the branches before I die!"

"Untangle yourself," said Medio Pollito. "I have no time to set you free. I'm off to see the world."

And hippity-hop he went through the dark woods, leaving the wind to die. "The very idea!" he thought. "If I stopped to help everybody who wanted helping, where would I be myself?"

The wood grew darker, and the night grew colder, and still Medio Pollito had seen nothing he had not seen before. "The world is wide," he said to himself. "I suppose one must travel a long way to find out what it is like."

The little half-chick was very tired. When he came to a bush, he hopped under it and went to sleep.

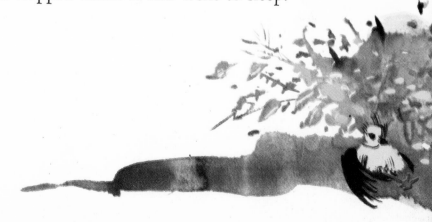

The next morning he awoke and went on with his
journey until he came to the edge of the woods. Far
away, in a city on a hill, the sun flashed on a tall, tall

tower. Medio Pollito knew that it could be none other than the tower of the king's castle.

Lifting his one wing, he gave a triumphant little crow.

"There is where I belong!" he crowed. "A distinguished chick like me belongs in the king's castle!"

And away he went until he came to the city where the castle stood.

That day it happened that the king was in a terrible temper. He wanted chicken for lunch, and there wasn't a chicken to be found anywhere. He raged and he stamped and he called the cook names. The cook was so frightened that he ran out of the castle and up and down the streets, hunting for a chicken. And just then Medio Pollito entered the city, looking for the king's castle. The cook grabbed him and ran home with him and threw him into the pot.

Now the water was in the pot, and the fire was under it, and when they saw Medio Pollito being thrown into the pot, the one began to boil and the other began to crackle. Medio Pollito was terribly frightened. "Help me! Help me!" he begged. "Water, don't drown me! Fire, don't burn me! If you do, I shall die."

"So?" said the fire. "When I was about to die, you would not fan me. Now I shall burn you to a crisp."

"And I," said the water, "shall drown you as soon as possible. When I was choking with sticks and leaves you would not help me. Why should I help you now?"

And the fire burned, and the water bubbled away until Medio Pollito was cooked black as a cinder.

Just then the cook looked in the pot and saw what had happened. "Oh, lack-a-luck!" he exclaimed. "This bird is burned to a crisp!" And he seized Medio Pollito by his one leg and threw him out the window.

As Medio Pollito sailed through the air, the wind caught him and whirled him around and around. "Stop! Stop!" he cried. "I am so dizzy I cannot catch my breath!"

But the wind only answered, "Hah! When I was caught in the trees, you would not free me. Do you think I will let you go, now that I have caught you at last?"

And the wind whirled him higher and higher until it had whirled him to the very top of the tallest steeple in the city, and there it left him.

If you visit the city of Madrid today, you can see Medio Pollito on top of the steeple. He turns when the wind blows, and that is all he can do. He has one leg

and one wing and one eye, and he is black as a cinder.
He is no longer called Medio Pollito. He is called
WEATHERCOCK!

A BRIDEGROOM FOR MISS MOUSE

by MAUNG HTIN AUNG

This story comes from Burma. Although the heroine is a mouse,
she might just as easily be the beautiful princess of European
fairy tales who marries the poor but worthy young man.

MISS Mouse was so beautiful that her mother and father
decided to marry her to the most powerful being on
earth. So they set out in search of a husband for their
daughter.

They went first to the Sun. "Oh, Sun," they begged, "please marry our beautiful daughter."

The Sun said he would be very happy to marry the beautiful Miss Mouse.

Now as soon as the Sun said he would marry their daughter, Mr. and Mrs. Mouse began to wonder if they had made a mistake. "Are you really the most powerful being on earth?" they asked.

"Why, no," replied the Sun, "the Rain is more powerful, because when it rains, I am driven from the sky."

"Sorry," said Mr. and Mrs. Mouse, "but we want only the most powerful being to marry our daughter."

They went to the Rain, but the Rain said the Wind was stronger than he, for rain clouds were always being driven about by the Wind.

"Sorry," said Mr. and Mrs. Mouse, "but we want only the most powerful being to marry our daughter."

So they went to the Wind, who said he would like to marry their daughter, but he was not the most powerful being. However hard he tried, he had never been able to blow away the Mountain that stood in his way.

So Mr. and Mrs. Mouse said, "Sorry," and went to the Mountain.

But the Mountain said he was not the most powerful being in the world. The Bull came every evening to sharpen his horns against the Mountain, and broke off great chunks of it, and the Mountain could do nothing to stop him.

So Mr. and Mrs. Mouse went to the Bull, who regretted to say that he was not the most powerful being. He had to turn right and left as the Rope ordered him.

So Mr. and Mrs. Mouse went to the Rope. The Rope was overjoyed at the idea of marrying the beautiful Miss Mouse, but he also had to admit that there was one more powerful than he, and that was the Mouse that lived in the cow shed. Every night the Mouse came to gnaw at the Rope, and the Rope could do nothing to stop him.

So the Mouse who lived in the cow shed was chosen as the bridegroom of Miss Mouse. He was a fine, handsome fellow, a good husband for beautiful Miss Mouse.